PHILIP K. DICK

# VULCAN'S HAMMER

Philip K. Dick was born in Chicago in 1928 and lived most of his life in California. He briefly attended the University of California, but dropped out before completing any classes. In 1952, he began writing professionally and proceeded to write numerous novels and short story collections. He won the Hugo Award for the best novel in 1962 for *The Man in the High Castle* and the John W. Campbell Memorial Award for best novel of the year in 1974 for *Flow My Tears, the Policeman Said*. Philip K. Dick died on March 2, 1982, in Santa Ana, California, of heart failure following a stroke.

## NOVELS BY PHILIP K. DICK

# VULCAN'S HAMMER

# VULCAN'S

# HAMMER

PHILIP K. DICK

VINTAGE BOOKS

A Division of Random House, Inc.

New York

FIRST VINTAGE BOOKS EDITION, AUGUST 2004

The Cataloging-in-Publication Data is on file
at the Library of Congress.

**Vintage ISBN: 1-4000-3012-9**

Book design by Christopher M. Zucker

www.vintagebooks.com

Printed in the United States of America
10  9  8  7  6  5  4  3  2  1

# VULCAN'S HAMMER

# CHAPTER ONE

Arthur Pitt was conscious of the mob as soon as he left the Unity office and started across the street. He stopped at the corner by his car and lit a cigarette. Unlocking the car, he studied the mob, holding his briefcase tightly.

There were fifty or sixty of them: people of the town, workers and small businessmen, petty clerks with steel-rimmed glasses. Mechanics and truckdrivers, farmers, housewives, a white-aproned grocer. The usual—lower middle-class, always the same.

Pitt slid into his car, and snapping on the dashboard mike, called his highest ranking superior, the South American Director. They were moving fast, now, filling up the street and surging silently toward him. They had, no doubt, identified him by his T-class clothes—white shirt and tie, gray suit, felt hat. Briefcase. The shine of his black shoes. The pencil beam gleaming in the breast pocket of his coat. He unclipped the gold tube and held it ready. *"Emergency,"* he said.

"Director Taubmann here," the dashboard speaker said. "Where are you?" The remote, official voice, so far up above him.

"Still in Cedar Groves, Alabama. There's a mob forming around me. I suppose they have the roads blocked. Looks like the whole town."

"Any Healers?"

Off to one side, on the curb, stood an old man with a massive head and short-cropped hair. Standing quietly in his drab brown robe, a knotted rope around his waist, sandals on his feet. "One," Pitt said.

"Try to get a scan for Vulcan 3."

"I'll try." The mob was all around the car now. Pitt could hear their hands, plucking and feeling at the car, exploring it carefully and with calm efficiency. He leaned back and double-locked the doors. The windows were rolled up; the hood was down tight. He snapped on the motor which activated the defense assembly built into the car. Beneath and around him the system hummed as its feedback elements searched for any weak links in the car's armor.

On the curb, the man in brown had not moved. He stood with a few others, people in ordinary street clothing. Pitt pulled the scanner out and lifted it up.

A rock at once hit the side of the car, below the window. The car shuddered; in his hands the scanner danced. A second rock hit directly against the window, sending a web of cracks rippling across it.

Pitt dropped the scanner. "I'm going to need help. They mean business."

"There's a crew already on the way. Try to get a better scan of him. We didn't get it well."

"Of course you didn't," Pitt said in anger. "They saw the thing in my hand and they deliberately let those rocks fly." One of the rear windows had cracked; hands groped blindly into the car. "I've got to get out of here, Taubmann." Pitt grinned bleakly as he saw, out of the corner of his eye, the car's assembly attempting to repair the broken window—attempting and failing. As new plastiglass foamed up, the alien hands grasped and wadded it aside.

"Don't get panicky," the tinny dashboard voice told him.

"Keep the old-brain down?" Pitt released the brake. The car moved forward a few feet and stopped dead. The motor died into silence, and with it, the car's defense system; the hum ceased.

Cold fear slid through Pitt's stomach. He gave up trying to find the scanner; with shaking fingers he lifted out his pencil beam. Four or five men were astride the hood, cutting off his view; others were on the cab above his head. A sudden shuddering roar: they were cutting through the roof with a heat drill.

"How long?" Pitt muttered thickly. "I'm stalled. They must have got some sort of interference plasma going—it conked everything out."

"They'll be along any minute," the placid, metallic voice said, lacking fear, so remote from him and his situation. The organization voice. Profound and mature, away from the scene of danger.

"They better hurry." The car shuddered as a whole barrage of rocks hit. The car tipped ominously; they were lifting it up on one side, trying to overturn it. Both back windows were out. A man's hand reached for the door release.

Pitt burned the hand to ash with his pencil beam. The stump frantically withdrew. "I got one."

"If you could scan some of them for us . . . "

More hands appeared. The interior of the car was sweltering; the heat drill was almost through. "I hate to do this." Pitt turned his pencil beam on his briefcase until there was nothing left. Hastily, he dissolved the contents of his pockets, everything in the glove compartment, his identification papers, and finally he burned his wallet. As the plastic bubbled away to black ooze, he saw, for an instant, a photograph of his wife . . . and then the picture was gone.

"Here they come," he said softly, as the whole side of the car crumpled with a hoarse groan and slid aside under the pressure of the drill.

"Try to hang on, Pitt. The crew should be there almost any—"

Abruptly the speaker went dead. Hands caught him, throwing him back against the seat. His coat ripped, his tie was pulled off. He screamed. A rock crashed into his face; the pencil beam fell to the floor. A broken bottle cut across his eyes and mouth. His scream bubbled into choked silence. The bodies scrambled over him. He sank down, lost in the clutching mass of warm-smelling humanity.

On the car's dashboard, a covert scanner, disguised as a cigar lighter, recorded the immediate scene; it continued to function. Pitt had not known about it; the device had come with the car supplied to him by his superiors. Now, from the mass of struggling people, a hand reached, expertly groped at the dashboard—tugged once, with great precision, at a cable. The covert scanner ceased functioning. Like Pitt, it had come to the end of its span.

Far off down the highway the sirens of the police crew shrieked mournfully.

The same expert hand withdrew. And was gone, back into the mass . . . once more mingled.

William Barris examined the photo carefully, once more comparing it with the second of scanning tape. On his desk his coffee cooled into muddy scum, forgotten among his papers. The Unity Building rang and vibrated with the sounds of endless calculators, statistics machines, vidphones, teletypes, and the innumerable electric typewriters of the minor clerks. Officials moved expertly back and forth in the labyrinth of offices, the countless cells in which T-class personnel worked. Three young secretaries, their high heels striking sharply, hurried past his desk, on their way back from their coffee break. Normally he would have taken notice of them, especially the slim blonde in the pink wool sweater, but today he did not; he was not even aware that they had passed.

"This face is unusual," Barris murmured. "Look at his eyes and the heavy ridge over the brows."

"Phrenology," Taubmann said indifferently. His plump, well-scrubbed features showed his boredom; *he* noticed the secretaries, even if Barris did not.

Barris threw down the photo. "No wonder they get so many followers. With organizers like that—" Again he peered at the tiny fragment of scanning tape; this was the only part that had been clear at all. Was it the same man? He could not be sure. Only a blur, a shape without features. At last he handed the photo back to Taubmann. "What's his name?"

"Father Fields." In a leisurely fashion, Taubmann thumbed through his file. "Fifty-nine years old. Trade: electrician. Top-grade turret-wiring expert. One of the best during the war. Born in Macon, Georgia, 1970. Joined the Healers two years ago, at the beginning. One of the founders, if you can believe the inform-ants involved here. Spent two months in the Atlanta Psycholog-ical Correction Labs."

Barris said, "That long?" He was amazed; for most men it took perhaps a week. Sanity came quickly at such an advanced lab—they had all the equipment he knew of, and some he had only glimpsed in passing. Every time he visited the place he had a deep sense of dread, in spite of his absolute immunity, the sworn sanctity that his position brought him.

"He escaped," Taubmann said. "Disappeared." He raised his head to meet Barris' gaze. "Without treatment."

"Two months there, and no treatments?"

"He was ill," Taubmann said with a faint, mocking smile. "An injury, and then a chronic blood condition. Then something from wartime radiation. He stalled—and then one day he was gone. Took one of these self-contained air-conditioning units off the wall and reworked it. With a spoon and a toothpick. Of course, no one knows what he made out of it; he took his results through the wall and yard and fence with him. All we had for our inspection were the leftover parts, the ones he didn't use." Taubmann returned the photo to the file. Pointing at the second of scanning tape he said, "If that's the same man, it's the first time we've heard anything about him since then."

"Did you know Pitt?"

"A little. Nice, rather naive young fellow. Devoted to his job. Family man. Applied for field duty because he wanted the extra monthly bonus. Made it possible for his wife to furnish her living room with Early New England oak furniture." Taubmann got to his feet. "The call is out for Father Fields. But of course it's been out for months."

"Too bad the police showed up late," Barris said. "Always a few minutes late." He studied Taubmann. Both of them, technically, were equals, and it was policy for equals in the organization to respect one another. But he had never been too fond of Taubmann; it seemed to him that the man was too concerned with his own status. Not interested in Unity for theoretical reasons.

Taubmann shrugged. "When a whole town's organized against you, it isn't so odd. They blocked the roads, cut wires and cables, jammed the vidphone channels."

"If you get Father Fields, send him in to me. I want to examine him personally."

Taubmann smiled thinly. "Certainly. But I doubt if we'll get him." He yawned and moved toward the door. "It's unlikely; he's a slick one."

"What do you know about this?" Barris demanded. "You seem familiar with him—almost on a personal basis."

Without the slightest loss of composure, Taubmann said, "I saw him at the Atlanta Labs. A couple of times. After all, Atlanta is part of my region." He met Barris' gaze steadily.

"Do you think it's the same man that Pitt saw slightly before his death?" Barris said. "The man who was organizing that mob?"

"Don't ask me," Taubmann said. "Send the photo and that bit of tape on to Vulcan 3. Ask it; that's what it's for."

"You know that Vulcan 3 has given no statement in over fifteen months," Barris said.

"Maybe it doesn't know what to say." Taubmann opened the door to the hall; his police bodyguard swarmed alertly around him. "I can tell you one thing, though. The Healers are after one thing and one thing only; everything else is talk—all this stuff about their wanting to destroy society and wreck civilization. That's good enough for the commercial news analysts, but we know that actually—"

"What are they really after?" Barris interrupted.

"They want to smash Vulcan 3. They want to strew its parts over the countryside. All this today, Pitt's death, the rest—they're trying to reach Vulcan 3."

"Pitt managed to burn his papers?"

"I suppose. We found nothing, no remains of him or any of his equipment." The door closed.

After he had waited a careful few minutes, Barris walked to the door, opened it and peered out to be sure that Taubmann had gone. Then he returned to his desk. Clicking on the closed-circuit vidsender he got the local Unity monitor. "Give me the Atlanta Psychological Correction Labs," he said, and then instantly he struck out with his hand and cut the circuit.

He thought, It's this sort of reasoning that's made us into the thing we are. The paranoid suspicions of one another. Unity, he thought with irony. Some unity, with each of us eyeing the other, watching for any mistake, any sign. Naturally Taubmann had contact with a major Healer; it's his job to interview any of them that fall into our hands. He's in charge of the Atlanta staff. That's why I consulted him in the first place.

And yet—the man's motives. He's in this for himself, Barris thought grimly. But what about mine? What are my motives, that lead me to suspect him?

After all, Jason Dill is getting along in years, and it will be one of us who will replace him. And if I could pin something on Taubmann, even the suspicion of treason, with no real facts . . .

So maybe my own shirts aren't so clean, Barris thought. I can't trust myself because I'm not disinterested—none of us are, in the whole Unity structure. Better not yield to my suspicions then, since I can't be sure of my motives.

Once more he contacted the local monitor. "Yes, sir," she said. "Your call to Atlanta—"

"I want that canceled," he said curtly. "Instead—" He took a deep breath. "Give me Unity Control at Geneva."

While the call was put through—it had to be cleared through

an assortment of desks along the thousands of miles of channel—he sat absently stirring his coffee. A man who avoided psychotherapy for two months, in the face of our finest medical men. I wonder if I could do that. What skill that must have taken. What tenacity.

The vidphone clicked. "Unity Control, sir."

"This is North American Director Barris." In a steady voice he said, "I wish to put through an emergency request to Vulcan 3."

A pause and then, "Any first-order data to offer?" The screen was blank; he got only the voice, and it was so bland, so impersonal, that he could not recognize the person. Some functionary, no doubt. A nameless cog.

"Nothing not already filed." His answer came with heavy reluctance. The functionary, nameless or not, knew the right questions; he was skilled at his job.

"Then," the voice said, "you'll have to put through your request in the usual fashion." The rustling of sheets of paper. "The delay period," the voice continued, "is now three days."

In a light, bantering voice, Barris said, "What's Vulcan 3 doing these days? Working out chess openings?" Such a quip *had* to be made in a bantering manner; his scalp depended on it.

"I'm sorry, Mr. Barris. The time lag can't be cut even for Director-level personnel."

Barris started to ring off. And then, plunging all the way into it, he said in a brisk, authoritative tone, "Let me talk to Jason Dill, then."

"Managing Director Dill is in conference." The functionary was not impressed, nor disturbed. "He can't be bothered in matters of routine."

With a savage swipe of his hand, Barris cut the circuit. The screen died. Three days! The eternal bureaucracy of the monster organization. They had him; they really knew how to delay.

He reflectively picked up his coffee cup and sipped it. The cold, bitter stuff choked him and he poured it out; the pot refilled the cup at once with fresh coffee.

Didn't Vulcan 3 give a damn? Maybe it wasn't concerned with the world-wide Movement that was out—as Taubmann had said—to smash its metal hide and strew its relays and memory tubes and wiring for the crows to pick over.

But it wasn't Vulcan 3, of course; it was the organization. From the vacant-eyed little secretaries off on their coffee breaks, all the way up through the managers to the Directors, the repairmen who kept Vulcan 3 going, the statisticians who collected data. And Jason Dill.

Was Dill deliberately isolating the other Directors, cutting them off from Vulcan 3? Perhaps Vulcan 3 had responded and the information had been withheld.

I'm suspecting even him, Barris thought. My own superior. The highest official in Unity. I must be breaking down under the strain; that's really insane.

I need a rest, he thought wildly. Pitt's death has done it; I feel somehow responsible, because after all I'm safe here, safe at this desk, while eager youngsters like that go out in the country, out where it's dangerous. They get it, if something goes wrong. Taubmann and I, all of us Directors—we have nothing to fear from those brown-robed crackpots.

At least, nothing to fear *yet*.

Taking out a request form, Barris began carefully to write. He wrote slowly, studying each word. The form gave him space for ten questions; he asked only two:

a) ARE THE HEALERS OF REAL SIGNIFICANCE?
b) WHY DON'T YOU RESPOND TO THEIR EXISTENCE?

Then he pushed the form into the relay slot and sat listening as the scanner whisked over its surface. Thousands of miles away, his questions joined the vast tide flowing in from all over the world, from the Unity offices in every country. Eleven Directorates— divisions of the planet. Each with its Director and staff and sub-directorate Unity offices. Each with its police organs under oath to the local Director.

In three days, Barris' turn would come and answers would flow back. His questions, processed by the elaborate mechanism, would be answered—eventually. As with everyone else in T-class, he submitted all problems of importance to the huge mechanical computer buried somewhere in the subsurface fortress near the Geneva offices.

He had no other choice. All policy-level matters were determined by Vulcan 3; that was the law.

Standing up, he motioned to one of the nearby secretaries who stood waiting. She immediately came toward his desk with her pad and writing stick. "Yes, sir," she said, smiling.

"I want to dictate a letter to Mrs. Arthur Pitt," Barris said. From his papers he gave her the address. But then, on second thought, he said, "No, I think I'll write it myself."

"In handwriting, sir?" the secretary said, blinking in surprise. "You mean the way children do in school?"

"Yes," he said.

"May I ask why, sir?"

Barris did not know; he had no rational reason. Sentimentality, he thought to himself as he dismissed the secretary. Throwback to the old days, to infantile patterns.

Your husband is dead in the line of duty, he said to himself as he sat at his desk meditating. Unity is deeply sorry. As Director, I wish to extend my personal sympathy to you in this tragic hour.

Damn it, he thought. I can't do it; I never can. I'll have to go and see her; I can't write a thing like this. There have been too many, lately. Too many deaths for me to stand. I'm not like Vulcan 3. I can't ignore it. I can't be silent.

And it didn't even occur in my region. The man wasn't even my employee.

Clicking open the line to his sub-Director, Barris said, "I want you to take over for the rest of today. I'm knocking off. I don't feel too well."

"Too bad, sir," Peter Allison said. But the pleasure was obvious, the satisfaction of being able to step from the wings and assume a more important spot, if only for a moment.

You'll have my job, Barris thought as he closed and locked his desk. You're gunning for it, just as I'm gunning for Dill's job. On and on, up the ladder to the top.

He wrote Mrs. Pitt's address down, put it in his shirt pocket, and left the office as quickly as he could, glad to get away. Glad to have an excuse to escape from the oppressive atmosphere.

# CHAPTER  TWO

Standing before the blackboard, Agnes Parker asked, "What does the year 1992 bring to mind?" She looked brightly around the class.

"The year 1992 brings to mind the conclusion of Atomic War

I and the beginning of the decade of international regulation," said Peter Thomas, one of the best of her students.

"Unity came into being," Patricia Edwards added. "Rational world order."

Mrs. Parker made a note on her chart. "Correct." She felt pride at the children's alert response. "And now perhaps someone can tell me about the Lisbon Laws of 1993."

The classroom was silent. A few pupils shuffled in their seats. Outside, warm June air beat against the windows. A fat robin hopped down from a branch and stood listening for worms. The trees rustled lazily.

"That's when Vulcan 3 was made," Hans Stein said.

Mrs. Parker smiled. "Vulcan 3 was made long before that; Vulcan 3 was made during the war. Vulcan 1 in 1970. Vulcan 2 in 1975. They had computers even before the war, in the middle of the century. The Vulcan series was developed by Otto Jordan, who worked with Nathaniel Greenstreet for Westinghouse, during the early days of the war . . ."

Mrs. Parker's voice trailed off into a yawn. She pulled herself together with an effort; this was no time to be dozing. Managing Director Jason Dill and his staff were supposed to be in the school somewhere, reviewing educational ideology. Vulcan 3 was rumored to have made inquiries concerning the school systems; it seemed to be interested in knowing the various value biases that were currently being formulated in the pupils' basic orientation programs. After all, it was the task of the schools, and especially the grammar schools, to infuse the youth of the world with the proper attitudes. What else were schools for?

"What," Mrs. Parker repeated, "were the Lisbon Laws of 1993? Doesn't anybody know? I really feel ashamed of you all, if you can't exert yourselves to memorize what may well be the most important facts you'll learn in your entire time of school. I suppose if you had your way you'd be reading those commercial comic books that teach adding and subtracting and other business crafts." Fiercely, she tapped on the floor with her toe. "Well? Do I hear an answer?"

For a moment there was no response. The rows of faces were blank. Then, abruptly, incredibly: "The Lisbon Laws dethroned God," a piping child's voice came from the back of the classroom. A girl's voice, severe and penetrating.

Mrs. Parker awoke from her torpor; she blinked in amazement. "Who said that?" she demanded. The class buzzed. Heads turned questioningly toward the back. "Who was that?"

"It was Jeannie Baker!" a boy hollered.

"It was not! It was Dorothy!"

Mrs. Parker paced rapidly down the aisle, past the children's desks. "The Lisbon Laws of 1993," she said sharply, "were the most important legislation of the past five hundred years." She spoke nervously, in a high-pitched shrill voice; gradually the glass turned toward her. Habit made them pay attention to her—the training of years. "All seventy nations of the world sent representatives to Lisbon. The world-wide Unity organization formally agreed that the great computer machines developed by Britain and the Soviet Union and the United States, and hitherto used in a purely advisory capacity, would now be given absolute power over the national governments in the determination of top-level policy—"

But at that moment Managing Director Jason Dill entered the classroom, and Mrs. Parker lapsed into respectful silence.

This was not the first time she had seen the man, the actual physical entity, in contrast to the synthetic images projected over the media to the public at large. And as before, she was taken by surprise; there was such a difference between the real man and his official image. In the back of her mind she wondered how the children were taking it. She glanced toward them and saw that all of them were gazing in awe, everything else forgotten.

She thought, He's actually not so different from the rest of us. The highest ranking human being . . . and he's just a plain man. An energetic middle-aged man with a shrewd face, twinkling eyes, and a genial smile of confidence. He's short, she thought. Shorter than some of the men around him.

His staff had entered with him, three men and two women, all in the businesslike T-class gray. No special badges. No royal gear. If I didn't know, she thought, I wouldn't guess. He's so unassuming.

"This is Managing Director Dill," she said. "The Coordinating Director of the Unity system." Her voice broke with tension. "Managing Director Dill is responsible only to Vulcan 3. No human being except Director Dill is permitted to approach the computer banks."

Director Dill nodded pleasantly to Mrs. Parker and to the class. "What are you children studying?" he asked in a friendly voice, the rich voice of a competent leader of the T-class.

The children shuffled shyly. "We're learning about the Lisbon Laws," a boy said.

"That's nice," Director Dill affirmed heartily, his alert eyes twinkling. He nodded to his staff and they moved back toward the door. "You children be good students and do what your teacher tells you."

"It was so nice of you," Mrs. Parker managed to say. "To drop by, so they could see you for a moment. Such an honor." She followed the group to the door, her heart fluttering. "They'll always remember this moment; they'll treasure it."

"Mr. Dill," a girl's voice came. "Can I ask you something?"

The room became abruptly silent. Mrs. Parker was chilled. *The voice.* The girl again. Who was it? Which one? She strained to see, her heart thumping in terror. Good lord, was that little devil going to say something in front of Director Dill?

"Certainly," Dill said, halting briefly at the door. "What do you want to ask?" He glanced at his wrist watch, smiling rather fixedly.

"Director Dill is in a hurry," Mrs. Parker managed to say. "He has so much to do, so many tasks. I think we had better let him go, don't you?"

But the firm little child's voice continued, as inflexible as steel. "Director Dill, don't you feel ashamed of yourself when you let a machine tell you what to do?"

Director Dill's fixed smile remained. Slowly, he turned away from the door, back toward the class. His bright, mature eyes roved about the room, seeking to pinpoint the questioner. "Who asked that?" he inquired pleasantly.

Silence.

Director Dill moved about the room, walking slowly, his hands in his pockets. He rubbed his chin, plucking at it absently. No one moved or spoke; Mrs. Parker and the Unity staff stood frozen in horror.

It's the end of my job, Mrs. Parker thought. Maybe they'll make me sign a request for therapy—maybe I'll have to undergo voluntary rehabilitation. No, she thought frantically. Please.

However, Director Dill was unshaken. He stopped in front of the blackboard. Experimentally, he raised his hand and moved it in a figure. White lines traced themselves on the dark surface. He made a few thoughtful motions and the date 1992 traced itself.

"The end of the war," he said.

He traced 1993 for the hushed class.

"The Lisbon Laws, which you're learning about. The year the combined nations of the world decided to throw in their lot together. To subordinate themselves in a realistic manner—not in the idealistic fashion of the UN days—to a common supranational authority, for the good of all mankind."

Director Dill moved away from the blackboard, gazing thoughtfully down at the floor. "The war had just ended; most of the planet was in ruins. Something drastic had to be done, because another war would destroy mankind. Something, some ultimate principle of organization, was needed. International control. Law, which no men or nations could break. Guardians were needed.

"But who would watch the Guardians? How could we be sure this supranational body would be free of the hate and bias, the animal passions that had set man against man throughout the centuries? Wouldn't this body, like all other man-made bodies, fall heir to the same vices, the same failings of interest over reason, emotion over logic?

"There was one answer. For years we had been using computers, giant constructs put together by the labor and talent of hundreds of trained experts, built to exact standards. Machines were free of the poisoning bias of self-interest and feeling that gnawed at man; they were capable of performing the objective calculations that for man would remain only an ideal, never a reality. If nations would be willing to give up their sovereignty, to subordinate their power to the objective, impartial directives of the—"

Again the thin child's voice cut through Dill's confident tone. The speech ceased, tumbled into ruin by the flat, direct interruption from the back of the classroom. "Mr. Dill, do you really believe that a machine is better than a man? That man can't manage his own world?"

For the first time, Director Dill's cheeks glowed red. He hesitated, half-smiling, gesturing with his right hand as he sought for words. "Well—" he murmured.

"I just don't know what to say," Mrs. Parker gasped, finding her voice. "I'm so sorry. Please believe me, I had no idea—"

Director Dill nodded understandingly to her. "Of course," he said in a low voice. "It's not your fault. These are not *tabulae rasae* which you can mold like plastic."

"Pardon?" she said, not understanding the foreign words. She had a dim idea that it was—what was it? Latin?

Dill said, "You will always have a certain number who will not respond." Now he had raised his voice for the class to hear. "I'm going to play a game with you," he said, and at once the small faces showed anticipation. "Now, I don't want you to say a word; I want you to clap your hands over your mouths and be the way our police crews are when they're waiting to catch one of the enemy." The small hands flew up to cover mouths; eyes shone with excitement. "Our police are so quiet," Dill continued. "And they look around; they search and search to see where the enemy is. Of course, they don't let the enemy know they're about to pounce."

The class giggled with joy.

"Now," Dill said, folding his arms. "We look around." The children dutifully peered around. "Where's the enemy? We count—one, two, three." Suddenly Dill threw up his arms and in a loud voice said, "And we *point* to the enemy. We point her *out!*"

Twenty hands pointed. In her chair in the back the small redhaired girl sat quietly, giving no reaction.

"What's your name?" Dill said, walking leisurely down the aisle until he stood near her desk.

The girl gazed silently up at Director Dill.

"Aren't you going to answer my question?" Dill said, smiling.

Calmly, the girl folded her small hands together on her desk. "Marion Fields," she said clearly. "And you haven't answered *my* questions."

Together, Director Dill and Mrs. Parker walked the corridor of the school building.

"I've had trouble with her from the start," Mrs. Parker said. "In fact, I protested their placing her in my class." Quickly, she said, "You'll find my written protest on file; I followed the regular method. I knew that something like this was going to happen, I just knew it!"

"I guarantee you," Director Dill said, "that you have nothing to fear. Your job is safe. You have my word." Glancing at the teacher he added reflectively, "Unless, of course, there's more to this than meets the eye." He paused at the door to the principal's office. "You have never met or seen her father, have you?"

"No," Mrs. Parker answered. "She's a ward of the government; her father was arrested and committed to the Atlanta—"

"I know," Dill interrupted. "She's nine, is she? Does she try to discuss current events with the other children? I presume that you have some manner of monitoring equipment going at all times—in the cafeteria and on the playground especially."

"We have complete tapes of all conversations among the pupils," Mrs. Parker said proudly. "There's never a moment when they're not overheard. Of course, we're so rushed and overworked, and our budget is so low . . . frankly, we've had trouble finding time to replay the tapes. There's a backlog, and all of us teachers try to spend at least an hour a day in careful replaying—"

"I understand," Dill murmured. "I know how overworked you all are, with all your responsibilities. It would be normal for any child her age to talk about her father. I was just curious. Obviously—" He broke off. "I believe," he said somberly, "that I'll have you sign a release permitting me to assume custody of her. Effective at once. Do you have someone you can send to her dorm to pick up her things? Her clothes and personal articles?" He glanced at his watch. "I don't have too much time."

"She has just the standard kit," Mrs. Parker said. "Class B, which is provided for nine-year-olds. That could be picked up anywhere. You can take her right—I'll have the form made out at once." She opened the door to the principal's office and waved to a clerk.

"You have no objection to my taking her?" Dill said.

"Certainly not," Mrs. Parker answered. "Why do you ask?"

In a dark, introspective voice, Dill said, "It would put an end to her schooling, for one thing."

"I don't see that that matters."

Dill eyed her, and she became flustered; his steady gaze made her shrink away. "I suppose," he said, "that schooling for her has been a failure anyhow. So it doesn't matter."

"That's right," she said quickly. "We can't help malcontents like her. As you pointed out in your statement to the class."

"Have her taken down to my car," Dill said. "She's been detained by someone capable of restraining her, I presume. It would be a shame if she selected this moment to sneak off."

"We have her locked in one of the washrooms," Mrs. Parker said.

Again he eyed her, but this time he said nothing. While she shakily made out the proper form he took a moment to gaze out the window at the playground below. Now it was recess; the faint, muffled voices of the children drifted up to the office.

"What game is that?" Dill said finally. "Where they mark with the chalk." He pointed.

"I don't know," she said, looking over his shoulder.

At that, Dill was dumbfounded. "You mean you let them play unorganized games? Games of their own devising?"

"No," she said. "I mean I'm not in charge of playground teaching; it's Miss Smollet who handles that. See her down there?"

When the custody transfer had been made out, Dill took it from her and departed. Presently she saw, through the window, the man and his staff crossing the playground. She watched as he waved genially to the children, and she saw him stop several times to bend down to speak to some individual child.

How incredible, she thought. That he could take the time for ordinary persons like us.

At Dill's car she saw the Fields girl. The small shape, wearing a coat, the bright red hair shimmering in the sun . . . and then an official of Dill's staff had boosted the child into the back of the car. Dill got in too, and the doors slammed. The car drove off. On the playground, a group of children had gathered by the high wire fence to wave.

Still trembling, Mrs. Parker made her way back up the corridor to her classroom. Is my job safe? she asked herself. Will I be investigated, or can I believe him? After all, he did give me his absolute assurance, and no one can contradict him. I know my record is clear, she thought desperately. I've never done anything subversive; I asked not to have that child in my class, and I never discuss current events in the classroom; I've never slipped once. But suppose—

Suddenly, at the corner of her eye, something moved.

She halted rigid where she was. A flicker of motion. Now gone. What was it? A deep, intuitive dread filled her; something had been there, near her, unobserved. Now swiftly vanished—she had caught only the most indistinct glimpse.

Spying on her! Some mechanism overhearing her. She was being watched. Not just the children, she thought in terror. But us, too. They have us watched, and I never knew for sure; I only guessed.

Could it read my thoughts? she asked herself. No, nothing can read thoughts. And I wasn't saying anything aloud. She looked up and down the corridor, striving to make out what it had been.

Who does it report to? she wondered. The police? Will they come and get me, take me to Atlanta or some place like that?

Gasping with fear, she managed to open the door of her classroom and enter.

# CHAPTER THREE

The Unity Control Building filled virtually the whole business area of Geneva, a great imposing square of white concrete and steel. Its endless rows of windows glittered in the late afternoon sun; lawns and shrubs surrounded the structure on all sides; gray-clad men and women hurried up the wide marble steps and through the doors.

Jason Dill's car pulled up at the guarded Director's entrance. He stepped quickly out and held the door open. "Come along," he said.

For a moment Marion Fields remained in the car, unwilling to leave. The leather seats had given her a sense of security, and she sat looking out at the man standing on the sidewalk, trying to control her fear of him. The man smiled at her, but she had no confidence in the smile; she had seen it too many times on the public television. It was too much a part of the world that she had been taught to distrust.

"Why?" she said. "What are you going to do?" But at last she slid slowly from the car onto the pavement. She was not sure where she was; the rapid trip had confused her.

"I'm sorry you had to leave your possessions behind," Dill said to her. He took hold of her hand and led her firmly up the steps of the great building. "We'll replace them," he said. "And we'll see that you have a pleasant time here with us; I promise you, on my word of honor." He glanced down to see how she was taking it.

The long echoing hall stretched out ahead of them, lit by recessed lights. Distant figures, tiny human shapes, scampered back and forth from one office to another. To the girl, it was like an even larger school; it was everything she had been subjected to but on a much larger scale.

"I want to go home," she said.

"This way," Dill said in a cheerful voice, as he guided her along. "You won't be lonely because there are a lot of nice people who work here who have children of their own, girls of their own. And they'll be glad to bring their children by so you can have someone to play with. Won't that be nice?"

"You can tell them," she said.

"Tell them what?" Dill said, as he turned down a side passage.

"To bring the children. And they will. Because you're the boss." She gazed up at him, and saw, for an instant, his composure depart. But almost at once he was smiling again. "Why do you always smile?" she said. "Aren't things ever bad, or aren't you able to admit it when they're bad? On the television you always say things are fine. Why don't you tell the truth?" She asked these questions with curiosity; it did not make sense to her. Surely he knew that he never told the truth.

"You know what I think's wrong with you, young woman?" Dill said. "I don't really think you're such a troublemaker as you pretend." He opened the door to an office. "I think you just worry too much." As he ushered her inside he said, "You should be like other children. Play more healthy outdoor games. Don't do so much thinking off by yourself. Isn't that what you do? Go off by yourself somewhere and brood?"

She had to nod in agreement. It was true.

Dill patted her on the shoulder. "You and I are going to get along fine," he said. "You know, I have two children of my own—a good bit older than you, though."

"I know," she said. "One's a boy and he's in the police youth, and your girl Joan is in the girls' army school in Boston. I read about it in a magazine they give us at school to read."

"Oh, yes," Dill murmured. "*World Today*. Do you like to read it?"

"No," she said. "It tells more lies even than you."

After that, the man said nothing; he concerned himself with papers on his desk, and left her to stand by herself.

"I'm sorry you don't like our magazine," he said finally, in a preoccupied voice. "Unity goes to a great deal of trouble to put it out. By the way, who told you to say that about Unity? Who taught you?"

"Nobody taught me."

"Not even your father?"

She said, "Do you know you're shorter than you look on television? Do they do that on purpose? Try to make you look bigger to impress people?"

To that, Dill said nothing. At his desk he had turned on a little machine; she saw lights flash.

"That's recording," she said.

Dill said, "Have you had a visit from your dad since his escape from Atlanta?"

"No," she said.

"Do you know what sort of place Atlanta is?"

"No," she said. But she did know. He stared at her, trying to see if she was lying, but she returned his stare. "It's a prison," she said at last. "Where they send men who speak their mind."

"No," Dill said. "It's a hospital. For mentally unbalanced people. It's a place where they get well."

In a low, steady voice, she said, "You're a liar."

"It's a psychological therapy place," Dill said. "Your father was—upset. He imagined all sorts of things that weren't so. There evidently were pressures on him too strong for him to bear, and so like a lot of perfectly normal people he cracked under the pressure."

"Did you ever meet him?"

Dill admitted, "No. But I have his record here." He showed her a great mass of documents that lay before him.

"They cured him at that place?" Marion asked.

"Yes," Dill said. But then he frowned. "No, I beg your pardon. He was too ill to be given therapy. And I see he managed to keep himself ill the entire two months he was there."

"So he isn't cured," she said. "He's still upset, isn't he?"

Dill said, "The Healers. What's your father's relationship to them?"

"I don't know."

Dill seated himself and leaned back in his chair, his hands behind his head. "Isn't it a little silly, those things you said? Overthrowing God . . . somebody has told you we were better off in the old days, before Unity, when we had war every twenty years." He pondered. "I wonder how the Healers got their name. Do you know?"

"No," she said.

"Didn't your father tell you?"

"No."

"Maybe I can tell you; I'll be a sort of substitute father, for a while. A 'healer' is a person who comes along with no degree or professional medical training and declares he can cure you by some odd means when the licensed medical profession has given you up. He's a quack, a crank, either an out-and-out nut or a cynical fake who wants to make some easy money and doesn't care how he goes about it. Like the cancer quacks— but you're too young; you wouldn't remember them." Leaning forward, he said, "But you may have heard of the radiation-sickness quacks. Do you remember ever seeing a man come by in an old car, with perhaps a sign mounted on top of it, selling bottles of medicine guaranteed to cure terrible radiation burns?"

She tried to recall. "I don't remember," she said. "I know I've seen men on television selling things that are supposed to cure all the ills of society."

Dill said, "No child would talk as you're talking. You've been trained to say this." His voice rose. "Haven't you?"

"Why are you so upset?" she said, genuinely surprised. "I didn't say it was any Unity salesman."

"But you meant us," Dill said, still flushed. "You meant our informational discussions, our public relations programs."

She said, "You're so suspicious. You see things that aren't there." That was something her father had said; she remembered that. He had said, *They're paranoids. Suspicious even of each other. Any opposition is the work of the devil.*

"The Healers," Dill was saying, "take advantage of the superstitions of the masses. The masses are ignorant, you see. They believe in crazy things: magic, gods and miracles, healing, the Touch. This cynical cult is playing on basic emotional hysterias familiar to all our sociologists, manipulating the masses like sheep, exploiting them to gain power."

"You have the power," she said. "All of it. My father says you've got a monopoly on it."

"The masses have a desire for religious certainty, the comforting balm of faith. You grasp what I'm saying, don't you? You seem to be a bright child."

She nodded faintly.

"They don't live by reason. They can't; they haven't the courage and discipline. They demand the metaphysical absolutes that started to go out as early as 1700. But war keeps bringing it back—the whole pack of frauds."

"Do you believe that?" she said. "That it's all frauds?"

Dill said, "I know that a man who says he has the Truth is a fraud. A man who peddles snake oil, like your—" He broke off. "A man," he said finally, "like your father. A spellbinder who fans up the flames of hate, inflames a mob until it kills."

To that she said nothing.

Jason Dill slid a piece of paper before her eyes. "Read this. It's about a man named Pitt—not a very important man, but it was worth your father's while to have him brutally murdered. Ever hear of him?"

"No," she said.

"Read it!" Dill said.

She took the report and examined it, her lips moving slowly.

"The mob," Dill said, "led by your father, pulled the man from his car and tore him to bits. What do you think of that?"

Marion pushed the paper back to him, saying nothing.

Leaning toward her, Dill yelled, "Why? What are they after? Do they want to bring back the old days? The war and hatred and international violence? These madmen are sweeping us back into the chaos and darkness of the past! And who gains? Nobody, except these spellbinders; they gain power. Is it worth it? Is it worth killing off half of mankind, wrecking cities—"

She interrupted, "That's not so. My father never said he was going to do anything like that." She felt herself become rigid with anger. "You're lying again, like you always do."

"Then what does he want? You tell me."

"They want Vulcan 3."

"I don't know what you mean." He scowled at her. "They're wasting their time. It repairs and maintains itself; we merely feed it data and the parts and supplies it wants. Nobody knows exactly where it is. Pitt didn't know."

"*You* know."

"Yes, I know." He studied her with such ferocity that she could not meet his gaze. "The worst thing that's happened to the world," he said at last, "in the time that you've been alive, is your father's escape from the Atlanta Psych Labs. A warped, psychopathic, deranged madman..." His voice sank to a mutter.

"If you met him," she said, "you'd like him."

Dill stared at her. And then, abruptly, he began to laugh. "Anyhow," he said when he had ceased laughing, "you'll stay here in the Unity offices. I'll be talking to you again from time to time. If we don't get results we can send you to Atlanta. But I'd rather not."

He stabbed a button on his desk and two armed Unity guards appeared at the office door. "Take this girl down to the third subsurface level; don't let anything happen that might harm her." Out of her earshot, he gave the guards instructions; she tried to hear but she could not.

I'll bet he was lying when he said there'd be other kids for me to play with, she thought. She had not seen another child yet, in this vast, forbidding building.

Tears came to her eyes, but she forced them back. Pretending to be examining the big dictionary in the corner of Director Dill's office, she waited for the guards to start ordering her into motion.

As Jason Dill sat moodily at his desk, a speaker near his arm said, "She's in her quarters now, sir. Anything else?"

"No," he said. Rising to his feet, he collected his papers, put them into his briefcase and left the office.

A moment later he was on his way out of the Unity Control Building, hurrying up the ramp to the confined field, past the nests of heavy-duty aerial guns and on to his private hanger. Soon he was heading across the early evening sky, toward the underground fortress where the great Vulcan computers were maintained, carefully hidden away from the race of man.

Strange little girl, he thought to himself. Mature in some ways, in others perfectly ordinary. How much of her was derived from her father? Father Fields secondhand, Dill thought. Seeing the man through her, trying to infer the father by means of the child.

He landed, and presently was submitting to the elaborate examination at the surface check-point, fidgeting impatiently. The tangle of equipment sent him on and he descended quickly into the depths of the underground fortress. At the second level he stopped the elevator and abruptly got off. A moment later he was standing before a sealed support-wall, tapping his foot nervously and waiting for the guards to pass him.

"All right, Mr. Dill." The wall slid back. Dill hurried down a long deserted corridor, his heels echoing mournfully. The air was clammy, and the lights flickered fitfully; he turned to the right and halted, peering into the yellow gloom.

There it was. Vulcan 2, dusty and silent. Virtually forgotten. No one came here anymore. Except himself. And even he not very often.

He thought, It's a wonder the thing still works.

Seating himself at one of the tables, he unzipped his briefcase and got out his papers. Carefully, he began preparing his questions in the proper manner; for this archaic computer he had to do the tape-feeding himself. With a manual punch, he spelled out on the iron oxide tape the first series, and then he activated the tape transport. It made an audible wheezing sound as it struggled into life.

In the old days, during the war, Vulcan 2 had been an intricate structure of great delicacy and subtlety, an elaborate instrument consulted by the skilled technicians daily. It had served Unity well, in its time; it had done honorable service. And, he thought, the schoolbooks still laud it; they still give it its proper credit.

Lights flashed, and a bit of tape popped from the slot and fell into the basket. He picked it up and read:

*Time will be required. Return in twenty-four hours, please.*

The computer could not function rapidly, now. He knew that, and this did not surprise him. Again taking up the punch, he made the balance of his questions into feeding data, and then, closing his brief case, he strode rapidly from the chamber, back up the musty, deserted corridor.

How lonesome it is here, he thought. No one else but me.

And yet—he had the sudden acute sensation that he was not alone, that someone was nearby, scrutinizing him. He glanced swiftly about. The dim yellow light did not show him much; he ceased walking, holding his breath and listening. There was no sound except the distant whirl of the old computer as it labored over his questions.

Lifting his head, Dill peered into the dusty shadows along the ceiling of the corridor. Strands of cobweb hung from the light fixtures; one bulb had gone dead, and that spot was black—a pit of total darkness.

In the darkness, something gleamed.

Eyes, he thought. He felt chill fear.

A dry, rustling noise. The eyes shot off; he saw the gleam still, retreating from him along the ceiling of the corridor. In an instant the eyes had gone. A bat? Bird of some sort, trapped down here? Carried down by the elevator?

Jason Dill shivered, hesitated, and then went on.

# CHAPTER FOUR

From Unity records, William Barris had obtained the address of Mr. and Mrs. Arthur Pitt. It did not surprise him to discover that the Pitts—now just Mrs. Pitt, he realized soberly—had a house in the expensive and fashionable Sahara region of North Africa. During the war that part of the world had been spared both hydrogen bomb explosions and fallout; now real estate there was priced out of the reach of most people, even those employed by the Unity system.

As his ship carried him from the North American landmass across the Atlantic, Barris thought, I wish I could afford to live there. It must have cost the man everything he had; in fact, he must have gone into debt up to his neck. I wonder why. Would it be worth it? Not to me, Barris thought. Perhaps for his wife . . .

He landed his ship at the fabulously illuminated Proust Field runways, and shortly thereafter he was driving by commercial robot taxi out the twelve-lane freeway to the Golden Lands Development, in which Mrs. Pitt lived.

The woman, he knew, had been notified already; he had made sure that he would not be bringing her the first news of her husband's death.

On each side of the road, orange trees and grass and sparkling blue fountains made him feel cool and relaxed. As yet there were no multiple-unit buildings; this area was perhaps the last in the world still zoned for one-unit dwellings only. The limit of luxury, he thought. One-unit dwellings were a vanishing phenomenon in the world.

The freeway branched; he turned to the right, following the sign. Presently SLOW warnings appeared. Ahead he saw a gate blocking the road; astonished, he brought his rented taxi to a halt. Was this development legally able to screen visitors? Apparently it was; the law sanctioned it. He saw several men in ornate uniforms—like ancient Latin American dictator garb— standing at stopped cars, inspecting the occupants. And, he saw, several of the cars were being turned back.

When the official had sauntered over to him, Barris said in a brusque voice, "Unity business."

The man shrugged. "Are you expected?" he asked in a bored tone.

"Listen," Barris began but the man was already pointing back at the through freeway. Subsiding, Barris said with great restraint, "I want to see Mrs. Arthur Pitt. Her husband was killed in the line of duty and I'm here expressing official regrets." That was actually not true, but it was near enough.

"I'll ask her if she wishes to see you," the uniformed man, heavy with medals and decorations, said. He took Barris' name; the fact that he was a Director did not seem to impress him. Going off, he spent some time at a portable vidscreen, and then he returned with a more pleasant expression on his face. "Mrs. Pitt is willing to have you admitted," he said. And the gate was drawn aside for Barris' rented taxi to pass.

Somewhat disconcerted by the experience, Barris drove on. Now he found himself surrounded by small, modern, brightly colored houses, all neat and trim, and each unique; he did not see two alike. He switched the automatic beam, and the taxi obediently hooked in to the circuit of the development. Otherwise, Barris realized, he would never find the house.

When the cab pulled over to the curb and stopped, he saw a slim, dark-haired young woman coming down the front steps of the house. She wore a wide-brimmed Mexican-style hat to protect her head from the midday African sun; from beneath the hat ringlets of black hair sparkled, the long Middle Eastern style so popular of late. On her feet she had sandals, and she wore a ruffled dress with bows and petticoats.

"I'm dreadfully sorry that you were treated that way, Director," she said in a low, toneless voice as he opened the door of the cab. "You understand that those uniformed guards are robots."

"No," he said. "I didn't know. But it isn't important." He surveyed her, seeing, he decided, one of the prettiest women that he had ever come across. Her face had a look of shock, a residue from the terrible news of her husband's death. But she seemed composed; she led him up the steps to the house walking very slowly.

"I believe I saw you once," she said as they reached the porch. "At a meeting of Unity personnel at which Arthur and I were present. You were on the platform, of course. With Mr. Dill."

The living room of the house, he noticed, was furnished as Taubmann had said. He saw Early New England oak furniture on every side.

"Please sit down," Mrs. Pitt said.

As he gingerly seated himself on a delicate-looking straight-backed chair, he thought to himself that for this woman being married to a Unity official had been a profitable career. "You have very nice things here," he said.

"Thank you," Mrs. Pitt said, seating herself opposite him on a couch. "I'm sorry," she said, "if my responses seem slow. When I got the news I had myself put under sedation. You can understand." Her voice trailed off.

Barris said, "Mrs. Pitt—"

"My name is Rachel," she said.

"All right," he said. He paused. Now that he was here, facing this woman, he did not know what to say; he was not sure, now, why he had come here.

"I know what's on your mind," Rachel Pitt said. "I put pressure on my husband to seek out active service so that we could have a comfortable home."

To that, Barris said nothing.

"Arthur was responsible to Director Taubmann," Rachel Pitt said. "I ran into Taubmann several times, and he made clear how he felt about me; it didn't particularly bother me at the time, but of course with Arthur dead—" She broke off. "It isn't true, of course. Living this way was Arthur's idea. I would have been glad to give it up any time; I didn't want to be stuck out here in this housing development, away from everything." For a moment she was silent. Reaching to the coffee table she took a package of cigarettes. "I was born in London," she said, as she lit a cigarette. "All my life I lived in a city, either in London or New York. My family wasn't very well off—my father was a tailor, in fact. Arthur's family has quite a good deal of money; I think he got his taste in interior decorating from his mother." She gazed at Barris. "This doesn't interest you. I'm sorry. Since I heard, I haven't been able to keep my thoughts in order."

"Are you all by yourself here?" he said. "Do you know anyone in the development?"

"No one that I want to depend on," she said. "Mostly you'll find ambitious young wives here. Their husbands all work for Unity; that goes without saying. Otherwise, how could they afford to live here?" Her tone was so bitter that he was amazed.

"What do you think you'll do?" he said.

Rachel Pitt said, "Maybe I'll join the Healers."

He did not know how to react. So he said nothing. This is a highly distraught woman, he thought. The grief, the calamity that she's involved in . . . or is she always like this? He had no way of telling.

"How much do you know about the circumstances surrounding Arthur's death?" she asked.

"I know most of the data," Barris said cautiously.

"Do you believe he was killed by—" She grimaced. "A mob? A

bunch of unorganized people? Farmers and shopkeepers, egged on by some old man in a robe?" Suddenly she sprang to her feet and hurled her cigarette against the wall; it rolled near him and he bent reflexively to retrieve it. "That's just the usual line they put out," she said. "I know better. My husband was murdered by someone in Unity—someone who was jealous of him, who envied him and everything he had achieved. He had a lot of enemies; every man with any ability who gets anywhere in the organization is hated." She subsided slightly, pacing about the room with her arms folded, her face strained and distorted. "Does this distress you?" she said at last. "To see me like this? You probably imagined some little clinging vine of a woman sobbing quietly to herself. Do I disappoint you? Forgive me." Her voice trembled with fury.

Barris said, "The facts as they were presented to me—"

"Don't kid me," Rachel said in a deadly, harsh voice. And then she shuddered and put her hands against her cheeks. "Is it all in my mind? He was always telling me about people in his office plotting to get rid of him, trying to get him in bad. Carrying tales. Part of being in Unity, he always said. The only way you can get to the top is push someone else away from the top." She stared at Barris wildly. "Who did you murder to get your job? How many men dead, so you could be Director? That's what Arthur was aiming for—that was his dream."

"Do you have any proof?" he said. "Anything to go on that would indicate that someone in the organization was involved?" It did not seem even remotely credible to him that someone in Unity could have been involved in the death of Arthur Pitt; more likely this woman's ability to handle reality had been severely curtailed by the recent tragedy. And yet, such things had happened, or at least so it was believed.

"My husband's official Unity car," Rachel said steadily, "had a little secret scanning device mounted on the dashboard. I saw the reports, and it was mentioned in them. When Director Taubmann was talking to me on the vidphone, do you know what I did? I didn't listen to his speech; I read the papers he had on his desk." Her voice rose and wavered. "One of the people who broke into Arthur's car knew about that scanner—*he shut it off.* Only someone in the organization could have known; even Arthur didn't know. It had to be someone up high." Her black eyes flashed. "Someone at Director level."

"Why?" Barris said, disconcerted.

"Afraid my husband would rise and threaten him. Jeopardize his job. Possibly eventually take his job from him, become Director in his place. Taubmann, I mean." She smiled thinly. "You know I mean him. So what are you going to do? Inform on me? Have me arrested for treason and carried off to Atlanta?"

Barris said, "I—I would prefer to give it some thought."

"Suppose you don't inform on me. I might be doing this to trap you, to test your loyalty to the system. You *have* to inform— it might be a trick!" She laughed curtly. "Does all this distress you? Now you wish you hadn't come to express your sympathy; see what you got yourself into by having humane motives?" Tears filled her eyes. "Go away," she said in a choked, unsteady voice. "What does the organization care about the wife of a dead minor petty fieldworker?"

Barris said, "I'm not sorry I came."

Going to the door, Rachel Pitt opened it. "You'll never be back," she said. "Go on, leave. Scuttle back to your safe office."

"I think you had better leave this house," Barris said.

"And go where?"

To that, he had no ready answer. "There's a cumbersome pension system," he began. "You'll get almost as much as your

husband was making. If you want to move back to New York or
London—"

"Do my charges seriously interest you?" Rachel broke in.
"Does it occur to you that I might be right? That a Director
might arrange the murder of a talented, ambitious underling to
protect his own job? It's odd, isn't it, how the police crews are
always just a moment late."

Shaken, ill-at-ease, Barris said, "I'll see you again. Soon, I
hope."

"Good-bye, Director," Rachel Pitt said, standing on the front
porch of her house as he descended the steps to his rented cab.
"Thank you for coming."

She was still there as he drove off.

As his ship carried him back across the Atlantic to North America, William Barris pondered. Could the Healers have contacts
within the Unity organization? Impossible. The woman's hyster-
ical conviction had overwhelmed him; it was her emotion, not
her reason, that had affected him. And yet he himself had been
suspicious of Taubmann.

Could it be that Father Fields' escape from Atlanta had been
arranged? Not the work of a single clever man, a deranged man
bent on escape and revenge, but the work of dull-witted officials
who had been instructed to let the man go?

That would explain why, in two long months, Fields had
been given no psychotherapy.

And now what? Barris asked himself acidly. Whom do I tell?
Do I confront Taubmann—with absolutely no facts? Do I go to
Jason Dill?

One other point occurred to him. If he ever did run afoul
of Taubmann, if the man ever attacked him for any reason, he

had an ally in Mrs. Pitt; he had someone to assist him in a counterattack.

And, Barris realized grimly, that was valuable in the Unity system, someone to back up your charges—if not with evidence, at least with added assertion. Where there's smoke there's fire, he said to himself. Someone should look into Taubmann's relationship with Father Fields. The customary procedure here would be to send an unsigned statement to Jason Dill, and let *him* start police spies to work tracing Taubmann, digging up evidence. My own men, Barris realized, could do it; I have good police in my own department. But if Taubmann got wind of it . . .

This is ghastly, he realized with a start. I have to free myself from this vicious cycle of suspicion and fear! I can't let myself be destroyed; I can't let that woman's morbid hysteria infiltrate my own thinking. Madness transmitted from person to person—isn't that what makes up a mob? Isn't that the group mind that we're supposed to be combatting?

I had better not see Rachel Pitt again, he decided.

But already he felt himself drawn to her. A vague but nonetheless powerful yearning had come into existence inside him; he could not pin down the mood. Certainly she was physically attractive, with her long dark hair, her flashing eyes, slender, active body. But she is not psychologically well-balanced, he decided. She would be a terrible liability; any relationship with a woman like that might wreck me. There is no telling which way she might jump. After all, her tie with Unity has been shattered, without warning; all her plans, her ambitions, have been thrown back in her teeth. She's got to find another entrée, a new technique for advancement and survival.

I made a mistake in looking her up, he thought. What would make a better contact than a Director? What could be of more use to her?

When he had gotten back to his own offices, he at once gave instructions that no calls from Mrs. Arthur Pitt be put through to him; any messages from her were to be put through proper channels, which meant that regular agencies—and clerks—would be dealing with her.

"A pension situation," he explained to his staff. "Her husband wasn't attached to my area, so there's no valid claim that can be filed against this office. She'll have to take it to Taubmann. He was her husband's superior, but she's got the idea that I can help in some way."

After that, alone in his office, he felt guilt. He had lied to his staff about the situation; he had patently misrepresented Mrs. Pitt in order to insure protection of himself. Is that an improvement? he asked himself. Is that my solution?

In her new quarters, Marion Fields sat listlessly reading a comic book. This one dealt with physics, a subject that fascinated her. But she had read the comic book three times, now, and it was hard for her to keep up an interest.

She was just starting to read it over for the fourth time when without warning the door burst open. There stood Jason Dill, his face white. "What do you know about Vulcan 2?" he shouted at her. "*Why did they destroy Vulcan 2?* Answer me!"

Blinking, she said, "The old computer?"

Dill's face hardened; he took a deep breath, struggling to control himself.

"What happened to the old computer?" she demanded, avid with curiosity. "Did it blow up? How do you know somebody did it? Maybe it just burst. Wasn't it old?" All her life she had read about, heard about, been told about, Vulcan 2; it was an historic shrine, like the museum that had been Washington, D.C. Except that all the children were taken to the Washington Museum to walk up and down the streets and roam in the great silent office buildings, but no one had ever seen Vulcan 2. "Can I look?" she demanded, following Jason Dill as he turned and started back out of the room. "Please let me look. If it blew up it isn't any good anymore anyhow, is it? So why can't I see it?"

Dill said, "Are you in contact with your father?"

"No," she said. "You know I'm not."

"How can I contact him?"

"I don't know," she said.

"He's quite important in the Healers' Movement, isn't he?" Dill faced her. "What would they gain by destroying a retired computer that's only good for minor work? Were they trying to reach Vulcan 3?" Raising his voice he shouted, "Did they think it was Vulcan 3? Did they make a mistake?"

To that, she could say nothing.

"Eventually we'll get him and bring him in," Dill said. "And this time he won't escape psychotherapy; I promise you that, child. Even if I have to supervise it myself."

As steadily as possible she said. "You're just mad because your old computer blew up, and you have to blame somebody else. You're just like my dad always said; you think the whole world's against you."

"The whole world is," Dill said in a harsh, low voice.

At that point he left, slamming the door shut after him. She stood listening to the sound of his shoes against the floor of the hall outside. Away the sound went, becoming fainter and fainter.

That man must have too much work to do, Marion Fields thought. They ought to give him a vacation.

# CHAPTER FIVE

There it was. Vulcan 2, or what remained of Vulcan 2—heaps of twisted debris; fused, wrecked masses of parts; scattered tubes and relays lost in random coils that had once been wiring. A great ruin, still smoldering. The acrid smoke of shorted transformers drifted up and hung against the ceiling of the chamber. Several technicians poked morosely at the rubbish; they had salvaged a few minor parts, nothing more. One of them had already given up and was putting his tools back in their case.

Jason Dill kicked a shapeless blob of ash with his foot. The change, the incredible change from the thing Vulcan 2 had been to *this,* still dazed him. No warning—he had been given no warning at all. He had left Vulcan 2, gone on about his business, waiting for the old computer to finish processing his questions . . . and then the technicians had called to tell him.

Again, for the millionth time, the questions scurried hopelessly through his brain. *How had it happened? How had they gotten it? And why?* It didn't make sense. If they had managed to locate and penetrate the fortress, if one of their agents had gotten this far, why had they wasted their time *here,* when Vulcan 3 was situated only six levels below?

Maybe they made a mistake; maybe they had destroyed the obsolete computer thinking it *was* Vulcan 3. This could have been an error, and, from the standpoint of Unity, a very fortunate one.

But as Jason Dill gazed at the wreckage, he thought, It doesn't look like an error. It's so damn systematic. So thorough. Done with such expert precision.

Should I release the news to the public? he asked himself. I could keep it quiet; these technicians are loyal to me completely. I could keep the destruction of Vulcan 2 a secret for years to come.

Or, he thought, I could say that Vulcan 3 was demolished; I could lay a trap, make them think they had been successful. Then maybe they would come out into the open. Reveal themselves.

They must be in our midst, he thought frantically. To be able to get in here—*they've subverted Unity.*

He felt horror, and, in addition, a deep personal loss. This old machine had been a companion of his for many years. When he had questions simple enough for it to answer he always came here; this visit was part of his life.

Reluctantly, he moved away from the ruins. No more coming here, he realized. The creaking old machine is gone; I'll never be using the manual punch again, laboriously making out the questions in terms that Vulcan 2 can assimilate.

He tapped his coat. They were still there, the answers that Vulcan 2 had given him, answers that he had puzzled over, again and again. He wanted clarification; his last visit had been to rephrase his queries, to get amplification. But the blast had ended that.

Deep in thought, Jason Dill left the chamber and made his way up the corridor, back to the elevator. This is a bad day for us, he thought to himself. We'll remember this for a long time.

Back in his own office he took time to examine the DQ forms that had come in. Larson, the leader of the data-feed team, showed him the rejects.

"Look at these." His young face stern with an ever-present awareness of duty, Larson carefully laid out a handful of forms.

"This one here—maybe you had better turn it back personally, so there won't be any trouble."

"Why do I have to attend to it?" Jason Dill said with irritation. "Can't you handle it? If you're overworked, hire a couple more clerks up here, from the pool. There's always plenty of clerks; you know that as well as I. We must have two million of them on the payrolls. And yet you still have to bother me." His wrath and anxiety swept up involuntarily, directed at his subordinate; he knew that he was taking it out on Larson, but he felt too depressed to worry about it.

Larson, with no change of expression, said in a firm voice, "This particular form was sent in by a Director. That's why I feel—"

"Give it to me, then," Jason Dill said, accepting it.

The form was from the North American Director, William Barris. Jason Dill had met the man any number of times; in his mind he retained an impression of a somewhat tall individual, with a high forehead . . . in his middle thirties, as Dill recalled. A hard worker. The man had not gotten up to the level of Director in the usual manner—by means of personal social contacts, by knowing the right persons—but by constant accurate and valuable work.

"This is interesting," Jason Dill said aloud to Larson; he put the form aside for a moment. "We ought to be sure we're publicizing this particular Director. Of course, he probably does a full public-relations job in his own district; we shouldn't worry."

Larson said, "I understand he made it up the hard way. His parents weren't anybody."

"We can show," Jason Dill said, "that the ordinary individual, with no pull, knowing no one in the organization, can come in

and take a regular low-grade job, such as clerk or even maintenance man, and in time, if he's got the ability and drive, he can
rise all the way up to the top. In fact, he might get to be Managing Director." Not, he thought to himself wryly, that it was such
a wonderful job to have.

"He won't be Managing Director for a while," Larson said, in
a tone of certitude.

"Hell," Jason Dill said wearily. "He can have my job right
now, if that's what he's after. I presume he is." Lifting the form
he glanced at it. The form asked two questions.

a) ARE THE HEALERS OF REAL SIGNIFICANCE?
b) WHY DON'T YOU RESPOND TO THEIR EXISTENCE?

Holding the form in his hands, Jason Dill thought, One of the
eternal bright young men, climbing rapidly up the Unity ladder.
Barris, Taubmann, Reynolds, Henderson—they were all making
their way confidently, efficiently, never missing a trick, never failing to exploit the slightest wedge. Give them an opportunity, he
thought with bitterness, and they'll knock you flat; they'll walk
right on over you and leave you there.

"Dog eat dog," he said aloud.

"Sir?" Larson said at once.

Jason Dill put down the form. He opened a drawer of his
desk and got out a flat metal tin; from it he took a capsule which
he placed against his wrist. At once the capsule dissolved
through the dermal layers; he felt it go into his body, passing into
his blood stream to begin work without delay. A tranquilizer . . .
one of the newest ones in the long, long series.

It works on me, he thought, and *they* work on me; it in one
direction, their constant pressure and harassment in the other.

Again Jason Dill picked up the form from Director Barris. "Are there many DQ's like this?"

"No, sir, but there is a general increase in tension. Several Directors besides Barris are wondering why Vulcan 3 gives no pronouncement on the Healers' Movement."

"They're all wondering," Jason Dill said brusquely.

"I mean," Larson said, "formally. Through official channels."

"Let me see the rest of the material."

Larson passed him the remaining DQ forms. "And here's the related matter from the data troughs." He passed over a huge sealed container. "We've weeded all the incoming material carefully."

After a time Jason Dill said, "I'd like the file on Barris."

"The documented file?"

Jason Dill said, "And the other one. The unsub-pak." Into his mind came the full term, not usually said outright. *Unsubstantiated.* "The worthless packet," he said. The phony charges, the trumped-up smears and lies and vicious poison-pen letters, mailed to Unity without signature. Unsigned, sometimes in the garbled prose of the psychotic, the lunatic with a grudge. And yet those papers were kept, were filed away. We shouldn't keep them, Jason Dill thought. Or make use of them, even to the extent of examining them. But we do. Right now he was going to look at such filth as it pertained to William Barris. The accumulation of years.

Presently the two files were placed before him on his desk. He inserted the microfilm into the scanner, and, for a time, studied the documented file. A procession of dull facts moved by; Barris had been born in Kent, Ohio; he had no brothers or sisters; his father was alive and employed by a bank in Chile; he had gone to work for Unity as a research analyst. Jason Dill speeded up the film, skipping about irritably. At last he rewound the microfilm and replaced it in the file. The man wasn't even married, he reflected; he led a routine life, one of virtue and work, if the documents could be believed. If they told the full story.

And now, Jason Dill thought, the slander. The missing parts; the other side, the dark shadow side.

To his disappointment, he found the unsub-pak on William Barris almost empty.

Is the man that innocent? Dill wondered. That he's made no enemies? Nonsense. The absence of accusation isn't a sign of the man's innocence; to rise to Director is to incur hostility and envy. Barris probably devotes a good part of his budget to distributing the wealth, to keeping everybody happy. And quiet.

"Nothing here," he said when Larson returned.

"I noticed how light the file felt," Larson said. "Sir, I went down to the data rooms and had them process all the recent material; I thought it possible there might be something not yet in the file." He added, "As you probably know, they're several weeks behind."

Seeing the paper in the man's hand, Jason Dill felt his pulse speed up in anticipation. "What came in?"

"This." Larson put down a sheet of what appeared to be expensive watermarked stationery. "I also took the measure, when I saw this, of having it analyzed and traced. So you'd know how to assess its worth."

"Unsigned," Dill said.

"Yes, sir. Our analysts say that it was mailed last night, some-where in Africa. Probably in Cairo."

Studying the letter, Jason Dill murmured, "Here's someone who Barris didn't manage to get to. At least not in time."

Larson said, "It's a woman's writing. Done with an ancient style of ball-point pen. They're trying to trace the make of pen. What you have there is actually a copy of the letter; they're still examining the actual document down in the labs. But for your purposes—"

"What are my purposes?" Dill said, half to himself. The letter was interesting, but not unique; he had seen such accusations made toward other officials in the Unity organization.

> *To whom it may concern:*
>
> *This is to notify you that William Barris, who is a Director, cannot be trusted, as he is in the pay of the Healers and has been for some time. A death that occurred recently can be laid at Mr. Barris' door, and he should be punished for his crime of seeing to it that an innocent and talented Unity servant was viciously murdered.*

"Notice that the writing slopes down," Larson said. "That's supposed to be an indication that the writer is mentally disturbed."

"Superstition," Dill said. "I wonder if this is referring to the murder of that fieldworker, Pitt. That's the most recent. What connection does Barris have with that? Was he Pitt's Director? Did he send him out?"

"I'll get all the facts for you, sir?" Larson said briskly.

After he had reread the unsigned letter, Jason Dill tossed it aside and again picked up the DQ form from Director Barris. With his pen he scratched a few lines on the bottom of the form. "Return this to him toward the end of the week. He failed to fill in his identification numbers; I'm returning it to be corrected."

Larson frowned. "That won't delay him much. Barris will immediately return the form correctly prepared."

Wearily, Jason Dill said, "That's my problem. You let me worry about it. Tend to your own business and you'll last a lot longer in this organization. That's a lesson you should have learned a long time ago."

Flushing, Larson muttered, "I'm sorry, sir."

"I think we should start a discreet investigation of Director Barris," Dill said. "Better send in one of the police secretaries; I'll dictate instructions."

While Larson rounded up the police secretary, Jason Dill sat gazing dully at the unsigned letter that accused Director Barris of being in the pay of the Healers. It would be interesting to know who wrote this, he thought to himself. Maybe we will know, someday soon.

In any case, there will be an investigation—of William Barris.


After the evening meal, Mrs. Agnes Parker sat in the school restaurant with two other teachers, exchanging gossip and relaxing after the long, tense day.

Leaning over so that no one passing by could hear, Miss Crowley whispered to Mrs. Parker, "Aren't you finished with that book, yet? If I had known it would take you so long, I wouldn't have agreed to let you read it first." Her plump, florid face trembled with indignation. "We really deserve our turn."

"Yes," Mrs. Dawes said, also leaning to join them. "I wish you'd go get it right now. Please let us have it, won't you?"

They argued, and at last Mrs. Parker reluctantly rose to her feet and moved away from the table, toward the stairway. It was a long walk up the stairs and along the hall to the wing of the building in which she had her own room, and once in the room she had to spend some time digging the book from its hiding place. The book, an ancient literary classic called *Lolita,* had been on the banned list for years; there was a heavy fine for any-one caught possessing it—and, for a teacher, it might mean a jail term. However, most of the teachers read and circulated such stimulating books back and forth among them, and so far no one had been caught.

Grumbling because she had not been able to finish the book, Mrs. Parker placed it inside a copy of *World Today* and carried it from her room, out into the hall. No one was in sight, so she continued on toward the stairway.

As she was descending she recalled that she had a job to do, a job that had to be done before morning; the little Fields girl's quarters had not been emptied, as was required by school law. A new pupil would be arriving in a day or so and would occupy the room; it was essential that someone in authority go over every inch of the room to be certain that no subversive or illicit articles belonging to the Fields girl remained to contaminate the new child. Considering the Fields girl's background, this rule was particularly important. As she left the stairway and hurried along a corridor, Mrs. Parker felt her heart skip several beats. She might get into a good deal of trouble by being forgetful in this area . . . they might think she wanted the new child contaminated.

The door to Marion Fields' old room was locked. How could that be? Mrs. Parker asked herself. The children weren't permitted keys; they could not lock any doors anywhere. It had to be one of the staff. Of course she herself had a key, but she hadn't had time to come down here since Managing Director Dill had taken custody of the child.

As she groped in her pocket for her master key, she heard a sound on the other side of the door. Someone was in the room.

"Who's in there?" she demanded, feeling frightened. If there was an unauthorized person in the room, she would get in trouble; it was her responsibility to maintain this dorm. Bringing her key out, she took a quick breath and then put the key into the lock. Maybe it's someone from the Unity offices checking up on me, she thought. Seeing what I let the Fields girl have in the way of possessions. The door opened and she switched on the light.

At first she saw no one. The bed, the curtains, the small desk in the corner . . . the chest of drawers!

On the chest of drawers something was perched. Something that gleamed, shiny metal, gleamed and clicked as it turned toward her. She saw into two glassy mechanical lenses, something with a tubelike body, the size of a child's bat, shot upward and swept toward her.

She raised her arms. *Stop,* she said to herself. She did not hear her voice; all she heard was a whistling noise in her ears, a deafening blast of sound that became a squeal. *Stop!* she wanted to scream, but she could not speak. She felt as if she were rising; now she had become weightless, floating. The room drifted into darkness. It fell away from her, farther and farther. No motion, no sound . . . just a single spark of light that flickered, hesitated, and then winked out.

Oh dear, she thought. I'm going to get into trouble. Even her thoughts seemed to drift away; she could not maintain them. I've done something wrong. This will cost me my job.

She drifted on and on.

# CHAPTER SIX

The buzzing of his bedside vidscreen woke Jason Dill from his deep, tranquilizer-induced sleep. Reaching, he reflexively snapped the line open, noticing as he did so that the call was on the private circuit. What is it now? he wondered, aware of a pervasive headache that he had been struggling with throughout hours of sleep. The time was late, he realized. At least four-thirty.

On the vidscreen an unfamiliar face appeared. He saw, briefly, a displayed identification-standard. The medical wing.

"Managing Director Dill," he muttered. "What do you want? Better check next time with the monitor; it's late at night here, even if it's noon where you are."

The medical person said, "Sir, I was advised by members of your staff to notify you at once." He glanced at a card. "A Mrs. Agnes Parker, a schoolteacher."

"Yes," Dill said, nodding.

"She was found by another teacher. Her spinal column had been damaged at several points and she died at 1:30 A.M. First examination indicated that the injuries were done deliberately. There's indication that some variety of heat plasma was induced. The spinal fluid evidently was boiled away by—"

"All right," Dill said. "Thanks for notifying me; you did absolutely right." Stabbing at a button he broke the connection and then asked the monitor for a direct line with Unity Police.

A placid, fleshy face appeared.

Dill said, "Have all the men guarding the Fields girl removed and a new crew, picked absolutely at random, put in at once.

Have the present crew detained until they can be fully cleared."
He considered. "Do you have the information regarding Agnes
Parker?"

"It came in an hour or two ago," the police official said.

"Damn it," Dill said. Too much time had passed. They could
work a lot of harm in that time. *They?*

The enemy.

"Any word on Father Fields?" he asked. "I take it for granted
you haven't managed to round him up yet."

"Sorry, sir," the police official said.

"Let me know what you find on the Parker woman," Dill
said. "Go over her file, naturally. I'll leave it to you; it's your business. It's the Fields girl I'm concerned about. Don't let anything
happen to her. Maybe you should check right now and see if
she's all right; notify me at once, either way." He rang off then
and sat back.

Were they trying to find out who took the Fields girl? he
asked himself. And where? That was no secret; she was loaded
into my car in broad daylight, in front of a playground of children.

They're getting closer, he said to himself. They got Vulcan 2
and they got that foolish, sycophantic schoolteacher whose idea
of taking care of her children was to gladly sign them over to the
first high official who came along. They can infiltrate our inner-
most buildings. They evidently know exactly what we're doing.
If they can get into the schools, where we train the youth to
believe . . .

For an hour or two he sat in the kitchen of his home, warm-
ing himself and smoking cigarettes. At last he saw the black night
sky begin to turn gray.

Returning to the vidscreen he called Larson. The man,
disheveled by sleep, peered at him grumpily until he recognized

his superior; then at once he became businesslike and polite. "Yes, sir," he said.

"I'm going to need you for a special run of questions to Vulcan 3," Jason Dill said. "We're going to have to prepare them with utmost care. And there will be difficult work regarding the data-feeding." He intended to go on, but Larson interrupted him.

"You'll be pleased to know that we have a line on the person who sent the unsigned letter accusing Director Barris," Larson said. "We followed up the lead about the 'talented murdered man.' We worked on the assumption that Arthur Pitt was meant, and we discovered that Pitt's wife lives in North Africa—in fact, she's in Cairo on shopping trips several times a week. There's such a high degree of probability that she wrote the letter that we're preparing an order to the police in that region to have her picked up. That's Blucher's region, and we'd better put it through his men so there won't be any hard feelings. I just want to get a clearance from you, so I won't have to assume the responsibility. You understand, sir. She may not have done it."

"Pick her up," Dill said, only half listening to the younger man's torrent of words.

"Right, sir," Larson said briskly. "And we'll let you know what we can get from her. It'll be interesting to see what her motive is for accusing Barris—assuming of course that it was she. My theory is that she may well be working for some other Director who—"

Dill broke the connection. And went wearily back to bed.

Toward the end of the week, Director William Barris received his DQ form back. Scrawled across the bottom was the notation: *"Improperly filled out. Please correct and refile."*

Furiously, Barris threw the form down on his desk and leaped to his feet. He snapped on the vidsender. "Give me Unity Control at Geneva."

The Geneva monitor formed. "Yes, sir?"

Barris held up the DQ form. "Who returned this? Whose writing is this? The feed-team leader?"

"No, sir." The monitor made a brief check. "It was Managing Director Dill who handled your form, sir."

Dill! Barris felt himself stiffen with indignation. "I want to talk to Dill at once."

"Mr. Dill is in conference. He can't be disturbed."

Barris killed the screen with a savage swipe. For a moment he stood thinking. There was no doubt of it; Jason Dill was stalling. I can't go on like this any further, Barris thought. I'll never get any answers out of Geneva this way. *What is Dill up to, for God's sake?*

Why is Dill refusing to cooperate with his own Directors?

Over a year, and no statement from Vulcan 3 on the Healers. Or had there been, and Dill hadn't released it?

With a surge of disbelief, he thought, Can Dill be keeping back information from the computer? Not letting it know what's going on?

Can it be that Vulcan 3 does not know about the Healers *at all?*

That simply did not seem credible. What ceaseless mass effort that would take on Dill's part; billions of data were fed to Vulcan 3 in one week alone; surely it would be next to impossible to keep all mention of the Movement from the great machine. And if any datum got in at all, the computer would react; it would note the datum, compare it with all other data, record the incongruity.

And, Barris thought, if Dill is concealing the existence of the Movement from Vulcan 3, what would be his motive? What would he gain by deliberately depriving himself—and Unity in general—of the computer's appraisal of the situation?

But that has been the situation for fifteen months, Barris realized. Nothing has been handed down to us from Vulcan 3, and either the machine has said nothing, or, if it has, Dill hasn't released it. So for all intents and purposes, the computer has *not* spoken.

What a basic flaw in the Unity structure, he thought bitterly. Only one man is in a position to deal with the computer, so that one man can cut us off completely; he can sever the world from Vulcan 3. Like some high priest who stands between man and god, Barris mused. It's obviously wrong. But what can we do? What can *I* do? I may be supreme authority in this region, but Dill is still my superior; he can remove me any time he wants. True it would be a complex and difficult procedure to remove a Director against his will, but it has been done several times. And if I go and accuse him of—

*Of what?*

He's doing something, Barris realized, but there's no way I can make out what it is. Not only do I have no facts, but I can't even see my way clearly enough to phrase an accusation. After all, I did fill out the DQ form improperly; that's a fact. And if Dill wants to say that Vulcan 3 simply has said nothing about the Healers, no one can contradict him because no one else has access to the machine. We have to take his word.

Barris thought, But I've had enough of taking his word. Fifteen months is long enough; the time has come to take action. Even if it means my forced resignation.

Which it probably will mean, and right away.

A job, Barris decided, isn't that important. You have to be able to trust the organization you're a part of; you have to believe in your superiors. If you think they're up to something, you have to get up from your chair and do something, even if it's nothing more than to confront them face-to-face and demand an explanation.

Reaching out his hand, he relit the vidscreen. "Give me the field. And hurry it up."

After a moment the field-tower monitor appeared. "Yes, sir?"

"This is Barris. Have a first-class ship ready at once. I'm taking off right away."

"Where to, sir?"

"To Geneva," Barris set his jaw grimly. "I have an appointment with Managing Director Dill." He added under his breath, "Whether Dill likes it or not."

As the ship carried him at high velocity toward Geneva, Barris considered his plans carefully.

What they'll say, he decided, is that I'm using this as a pretext to embarrass Jason Dill. That I'm not sincere; that in fact I'm using the silence of Vulcan 3 as a device to make a bid for Jason Dill's job. My coming to Geneva will just go to prove how ruthlessly ambitious I am. And I won't be able to disprove the charge; I have no way by which I can prove that my motives are pure.

This time the chronic doubt did not assail him; he *knew* that he was acting for the good of the organization. I know my own mind this time, he realized. In this case I can trust myself.

I'll just have to stand firm, he told himself. If I keep denying that I'm trying to undercut Dill for personal advantage—

But he knew better. All the denials in the world won't help me, he thought, once they loose the gods. They can get a couple of those police psychologists up from Atlanta, and once those boys have gone over me I'll *agree* with my accusers; I'll be convinced that I'm cynically exploiting Dill's problems and undermining the organization. They'll even have me convinced that I'm a traitor and ought to be sentenced to forced labor on Luna.

At the thought of the Atlanta psychologists, he felt cold perspiration stand out on his throat and forehead.

Only once had he been up against them, and that was the third year of his employment with Unity. Some unbalanced clerk in his department—at that time he had managed a small rural branch of Unity—had been caught stealing Unity property and reselling it on the black market. Unity of course had a monopoly on advanced technological equipment, and certain items were excessively valuable. It was a constant temptation, and this particular clerk had been in charge of inventories; the temptation had been coupled with opportunity, and the two together had been too much. The secret police had caught up with the man almost at once, had arrested him and gained the usual confession. To get himself in good, or what he imagined to be in good, the man had implicated several others in the branch office, including William Barris. And so a warrant had been served on him, and he had been hauled down in the middle of the night for an "interview."

There was no particular onus connected with being served with a police warrant; virtually every citizen became involved with the police at one time or another in his life. The incident had not hurt Barris' career; he had very quickly been released, and he had gone on at his job, and no one had brought the matter up when time came for his advancement to a high position.

But for half an hour at police headquarters he had been worked over by two psychologists, and the memory was still with him to wake him up late at night—a bad dream but unfortunately one that might recur in reality at any time.

If he were to step out of line even now, in his position as North American Director with supreme authority over the area north of the Mason-Dixon Line . . .

And, as he was carried closer and closer to Unity Control at Geneva, he was decidedly sticking his neck out. *I should mind my own business,* he told himself. That is a rule we all learn, if we expect to get up the ladder or even keep out of jail.

But this *is* my business!

Not much later a recorded voice said pleasantly, "We are about to land, Mr. Barris."

Geneva lay below. The ship was descending, pulled down by the automatic relays that had guided it from his field, across the Atlantic and over Western Europe.

Barris thought, Probably they already know I'm on my way. Some flunky, some minor informant, has relayed the information. Undoubtedly some petty clerk in my own building is a spy for Unity Control.

And now, as he rose from his chair and moved toward the exit, someone else was no doubt waiting at the Geneva terminal, watching to mark his arrival. I'll be followed the entire time, he decided.

At the exit he hesitated. I can turn around and go back, he said to himself. I can pretend I never started this trip, and probably no one will ever bring it up; they will know I started to come here, got as far as the field, but they won't know why. They'll never be able to establish that I intended to confront my superior, Jason Dill.

He hesitated, and then he touched the stud that opened the

door. It swung aside, and bright midday sunlight spilled into the small ship. Barris filled his lungs with fresh air, paused, and then descended the ramp to the field.

As he walked across the open space toward the terminal building, a shape standing by the fence detached itself. There's one, he realized. Watching for me. The shape moved slowly toward him. It was a figure in a long blue coat. A woman, her hair up in a bandanna, her hands in her coat pockets. He did not recognize her. Sharp pale features. Such intense eyes, he thought. Staring at him. She did not speak or show any expression until the two of them were separated by only a few feet. And then her colorless lips moved.

"Don't you remember me, Mr. Barris?" she said in a hollow voice. She fell in beside him and walked along with him, toward the terminal building. "I'd like to talk to you. I think it'll be worth your while."

He said, "Rachel Pitt."

Glancing at him, Rachel said, "I have something to sell. A piece of news that could determine your future." Her voice was hard and thin, as brittle as glass. "But I have to have something back; I need something in exchange."

"I don't want to do any business with you," he said. "I didn't come here to see you."

"I know," she said. "I tried to get hold of you at your office; they stalled me every time. I knew right away that you had given orders to that effect."

Barris said nothing. This is really bad, he thought. That this demented woman should manage to locate me, here, at this time.

"You're not interested," Rachel said, "and I know why not; all you can think of is how successfully you're going to deal with Jason Dill. But you see, you won't be able to deal with him at all."

"Why not?" he said, trying to keep any emotions he might be feeling out of his voice.

Rachel said, "I've been under arrest for a couple of days, now. They had me picked up and brought here."

"I wondered what you were doing here," he said.

"A loyal Unity wife," she said. "Devoted to the organization. Whose husband was killed only a few—" She broke off. "But you don't care about that, either." At the fence she halted, facing him. "You can either go directly to the Unity Control Building, or you can take half an hour and spend it with me. I advise the latter. If you decide to go on and see Dill now, without hearing me out . . ." She shrugged. "I can't stop you. Go ahead." Her black eyes glowed unwinkingly as she waited.

This woman is really out of her mind, Barris thought. The rigid, fanatical expression . . . But even so, could he afford to ignore her?

"Do you think I'm trying to seduce you?" she said.

Startled, he said, "I—"

"I mean, seduce you away from your high purpose." For the first time she smiled and seemed to relax. "Mr. Barris," she said with a shudder. "I'll tell you the truth. I've been under intensive examination for two days, now. You can suppose who by. But it doesn't matter. Why should I care? After what's happened to me . . ." Her voice trailed off, then resumed. "Do you think I escaped? That they're after me?" A mocking, bantering irony danced in her eyes. "Hell no. They let me go. They gave me compulsive psychotherapy for two days, and then they told me I could go home; they shoved me out the door."

A group of people passed by on their way to a ship; Barris and Rachel were both silent for a time.

"Why did they haul you in?" he asked finally.

Rachel said, "Oh, I was supposed to have written some kind of a poison-pen letter, accusing someone high up in Unity. I managed to convince them I was innocent—or rather, their analysis of the contents of my mind convinced them; all I did was sit. They took my mind out, took it apart, studied it, put the pieces back together and stuffed them back in my head." Reaching up, she slid aside the bandanna for a moment; he saw, with grim aversion, the neat white scar slightly before her hairline. "It's all back," she said. "At least, I hope it is."

With compassion, he said, "That's really terrible. A real abuse of human beings. It should be stopped."

"If you get to be Managing Director, maybe you can stop it," she said. "Who knows? You might someday be—after all, you're bright and hardworking and ambitious. All you have to do is defeat all those other bright, hardworking, ambitious Directors. Like Taubmann."

"Is he the one you're supposed to have accused?" Barris said.

"No," she said, in a faint voice. "It's you, William Barris. Isn't that interesting? Anyhow, now I've given you my news—free. There's a letter in Jason Dill's file accusing you of being in the pay of the Healers; they showed it to me. Someone is trying to get you, and Dill is interested. Isn't that worth your knowing, before you go in there and lock horns with him?"

Barris said, "How do you know I'm here to do that?"

Her dark eyes flickered. "Why else would you be here?" But her voice had a faltering tone now.

Reaching out, he took hold of her arm. With firmness, he guided her along the walk to the street side of the field. "I will take the time to talk to you," he said. He racked his mind, trying to think of a place to take her. Already they had come to the public taxi stand; a robot cab had spotted them and was rolling in their direction.

The door of the cab opened. The mechanical voice said, "May I be of service, please?"

Barris slid into the cab and drew the woman in beside him. Still holding firmly onto her, he said to the cab, "Say listen, can you find us a hotel, not too conspicuous—you know." He could hear the receptor mechanism of the cab whirring as it responded. "For us to get a load off our feet," he said. "My girl and me. You know."

Presently the cab said, "Yes, sir." It began to move along the busy Geneva streets. "Out-of-the-way hotel where you will find the privacy you desire." It added, "The Hotel Bond, sir."

Rachel Pitt said nothing; she stared sightlessly ahead.

# CHAPTER SEVEN

In his pockets, Jason Dill carried the two reels of tape; they never left him, night and day. He had them with him now as he walked slowly along the brightly lit corridor. Once again, involuntarily, he lifted his hand and rubbed the bulge which the tapes made. Like a magic charm, he thought to himself with irony. And we accuse the masses of being superstitious!

Ahead of him, lights switched on. Behind him, enormous reinforced doors slid shut to fill in the chamber's single entrance. The huge calculator rose in front of him, the immense tower of receptor banks and indicators. He was alone with it—alone with Vulcan 3.

Very little of the computer was visible; its bulk disappeared into regions which he had never seen, which in fact no human had ever seen. During the course of its existence it had expanded certain portions of itself. To do so it had cleared away the granite and shale earth; it had, for a long time now, been conducting excavation operations in the vicinity. Sometimes Jason Dill could hear that sound going on like a far-off, incredibly high-pitched dentist's drill. Now and then he had listened and tried to guess where the operations were taking place. It was only a guess. Their only check on the growth and development of Vulcan 3 lay in two clues: the amount of rock thrown up to the surface, to be carted off, and the variety, amount, and nature of the raw materials and tools and parts which the computer requested.

Now, as Jason Dill stood facing the thing, he saw that it had put forth a new reel of supply requisitions; it was there for him to pick up and fill. As if, he thought, I'm some errand boy.

I do its shopping, he realized. It's stuck here, so I go out and come back with the week's groceries. Only in its case we don't supply food; we supply just about everything else but.

The financial cost of supporting Vulcan 3 was immense. Part of the taxation program conducted by Unity on a worldwide basis existed to maintain the computer. At the latest estimate, Vulcan 3's share of the taxes came to about forty-three percent.

And the rest, Dill thought idly, goes to schools, for roads, hospitals, fire departments, police—the lesser order of human needs.

Beneath his feet the floor vibrated. This was the deepest level which the engineers had constructed, and yet something was constantly going on below. He had felt the vibrations before. What lay down there? No black earth; not the inert ground. Energy, tubes and pipes, wiring, transformers, self-contained machinery . . . He had a mental image of relentless activity going on: carts carrying supplies in, wastes out; lights blinking on and off; relays closing; switches cooling and reheating; worn-out parts replaced; new parts invented; superior designs replacing obsolete designs. And how far had it spread? Miles? Were there even more levels beneath the one transmitting up through the soles of his shoes? Did it go down, down, *forever?*

Vulcan 3 was aware of him. Across the vast impersonal face of metal an acknowledgment gleamed, a ribbon of fluid letters that appeared briefly and then vanished. Jason Dill had to catch the words at once or not at all; no latitude for human dullness was given.

*Is the educational bias survey complete?*

"Almost," Dill said. "A few more days." As always, in dealing with Vulcan 3, he felt a deep, inertial reluctance; it slowed his responses and hung over his mind, his faculties, like a dead weight. In the presence of the computer he found himself becoming stupid. He always gave the shortest answers; it was easier. And as soon as the first words lit up in the air above his head, he had a desire to leave; already, he wanted to go.

But this was his job, this being cloistered here with Vulcan 3. Someone had to do it. Some human being had to stand in this spot.

He had never had this feeling in the presence of Vulcan 2.

Now, new words formed, like lightning flashing blue-white in the damp air.

*I need it at once.*

"It'll be along as soon as the feed-teams can turn it into data forms."

Vulcan 3 was—well, he thought, the only word was *agitated.* Power lines glowed red—the origin of the series' name. The rumblings and dull flashes of red had reminded Nathaniel

Greenstreet of the ancient god's forge, the lame god who had created the thunderbolts for Jupiter, in an age long past.

*There is some element misfunctioning. A significant shift in the orientation of certain social strata which cannot be explained in terms of data already available to me. A realignment of the social pyramid is forming in response to historic-dynamic factors unfamiliar to me. I must know more if I am to deal with this.*

A faint tendril of alarm moved through Jason Dill. What did Vulcan 3 suspect? "All data is made available to you as soon as possible."

*A decided bifurcation of society seems in the making. Be certain your report on educational bias is complete. I will need all the relevant facts.*

After a pause, Vulcan 3 added: *I sense a rapidly approaching crisis.*

"What kind of crisis?" Dill demanded nervously.

*Ideological. A new orientation appears to be on the verge of verbalization. A Gestalt derived from the experience of the lowest classes. Reflecting their dissatisfaction.*

"Dissatisfaction? With what?"

*Essentially, the masses reject the concept of stability. In the main, those without sufficient property to be firmly rooted are more concerned with gain than with security. To them, society is an arena of adventure. A structure in which they hope to rise to a superior power status.*

"I see," Dill said dutifully.

*A rationally controlled, stable society such as ours defeats their desires. In a rapidly altering, unstable society the lowest classes would stand a good chance of seizing power. Basically, the lowest classes are adventurers, conceiving life as a gamble, a game rather than a task, with social power as the stakes.*

"Interesting," Dill said. "So for them the concept of luck plays a major role. Those on top have had good luck. Those—" But Vulcan 3 was not interested in his contribution; it had already continued.

*The dissatisfaction of the masses is not based on economic deprivation but on a sense of ineffectuality. Not an increased standard of living, but more social power, is their fundamental goal. Because of their emotional orientation, they arise and act when a powerful leader-figure can coordinate them into a functioning unit rather than a chaotic mass of unformed elements.*

Dill had no reply to that. It was evident that Vulcan 3 had sifted the information available, and had come up with uncomfortably close inferences. That, of course, was the machine's forte; basically it was a device par excellence for performing the processes of deductive and inductive reasoning. It ruthlessly passed from one step to the next and arrived at the correct inference, whatever it was.

Without direct knowledge of any kind, Vulcan 3 was able to deduce, from general historic principles, the social conflicts developing in the contemporary world. It had manufactured a picture of the situation which faced the average human being as he woke up in the morning and reluctantly greeted the day. Stuck down here, Vulcan 3 had, through indirect and incomplete evidence, *imagined* things as they actually were.

Sweat came out on Dill's forehead. He was dealing with a mind greater than any one man's or any group of men's. This proof of the prowess of the computer—this verification of Greenstreet's notion that a machine was not limited merely to doing what man could do, but doing it faster . . . Vulcan 3 was patently doing what a man could *not* do no matter how much time he had available to him.

Down here, buried underground in the dark, in this constant

isolation, a human being would go mad; he would lose all contact with the world, all ideas of what was going on. As time progressed he would develop a less and less accurate picture of reality; he would become progressively more hallucinated. Vulcan 3, however, moved continually in the opposite direction; it was, in a sense, moving by degrees toward inevitable *sanity,* or at least maturity—if, by that, was meant a clear, accurate, and full picture of things as they really were. A picture, Jason Dill realized, that no human being has ever had or will ever have. All humans are partial. And this giant is not!

"I'll put a rush on the educational survey," he murmured. "Is there anything else you need?"

*The statistical report on rural linguistics has not come in. Why is that? It was under the personal supervision of your subcoordinator, Arthur Graveson Pitt.*

Dill cursed silently. Good lord! Vulcan 3 never mislaid or lost or mistook a single datum among the billions that it ingested and stored away. "Pitt was injured," Dill said aloud, his mind racing desperately. "His car overturned on a winding mountain road in Colorado. Or at least that's the way I recall it. I'd have to check to be sure, but—"

*Have his report completed by someone else. I require it. Is his injury serious?*

Dill hesitated. "As a matter of fact, they don't think he'll live. They say—"

*Why have so many T-class persons been killed in the past year? I want more information on this. According to my statistics only one-fifth of that number should have died of natural causes. Some vital factor is missing. I must have more data.*

"All right," Dill muttered. "We'll get you more data; anything you want."

*I am considering calling a special meeting of the Control Council. I am on the verge of deciding to question the staff of eleven Regional Directors personally.*

At that Dill was stunned; he tried to speak, but for a time he could not. He could only stare fixedly at the ribbon of words. The ribbon moved inexorably on.

*I am not satisfied with the way data is supplied. I may demand your removal and an entirely new system of feeding.*

Dill's mouth opened and closed. Aware that he was shaking visibly, he backed away from the computer. "Unless you want something else," he managed, "I have business. In Geneva." All he wanted to do was get out of the situation, away from the chamber.

*Nothing more. You may go.*

As quickly as possible, Dill left the chamber, ascending by express lift to the surface level. Around him, in a blur, guards checked him over; he was scarcely aware of them.

What a going-over, he thought. What an ordeal. Talk about the Atlanta psychologists—they're nothing compared with what I have to face, day after day.

God, how I hate that machine, he thought. He was still trembling, his heart palpitating; he could not breathe, and for a time he sat on a leather-covered couch in the outer lounge, recovering.

To one of the attendants he said, "I'd like a glass of some stimulant. Anything you have."

Presently it was in his hand, a tall green glass; he gulped it down and felt a trifle better. The attendant was waiting around to be paid, he realized; the man had a tray and a bill.

"Seventy-five cents, sir," the attendant said.

To Dill it was the final blow. His position as Managing Director did not exempt him from these annoyances; he had to fish around in his pocket for change. And meanwhile, he thought, the future of our society rests with me. While I dig up seventy-five cents for this idiot.

I ought to let them all get blown to bits. *I ought to give up.*

William Barris felt a little more relaxed as the cab carried him and Rachel Pitt into the dark, overpopulated, older section of the city. On the sidewalks clumps of elderly men in seedy garments and battered hats stood inertly. Teenagers lounged by store windows. Most of the store windows, Barris noticed, had metal bars or gratings protecting their displays from theft. Rubbish lay piled up in alleyways.

"Do you mind coming here?" he asked the woman beside him. "Or is it too depressing?"

Rachel had taken off her coat and put it across her lap. She wore a short-sleeved cotton shirt, probably the one she had had on when the police arrested her; it looked to him like something more suited for house use. And, he saw, her throat was streaked with what appeared to be dust. She had a tired, wan expression and she sat listlessly.

"You know, I like the city," she said, after a time.

"Even this part?"

"I've been staying in this section," she said. "Since they let me go."

Barris said, "Did they give you time to pack? Were you able to take any clothes with you?"

"Nothing," she said.

"What about money?"

"They were very kind." Her voice had weary irony in it. "No, they didn't let me take any money; they simply bundled me into a police ship and took off for Europe. But before they let me go they permitted me to draw enough money from my husband's pension payment to take care of getting me back home." Turning her head she finished, "Because of all the red tape, it will be several months before the regular payments will be forthcoming. This was a favor they did me."

To that, Barris could say nothing.

"Do you think," Rachel said, "that I resent the way Unity has treated me?"

"Yes," he said.

Rachel said, "You're right."

Now the cab had begun to coast up to the entrance of an ancient brick hotel with a tattered awning. Feeling somewhat dismayed by the appearance of the Bond Hotel, Barris said, "Will this be all right, this place?"

"Yes," Rachel said. "In fact, this is where I would have had the cab take us. I had intended to bring you here."

The cab halted and its door swung open. As Barris paid it, he thought, Maybe I shouldn't have let it decide for me. Maybe I ought to get back in and have it drive on. Turning, he glanced up at the hotel.

Rachel Pitt had already started up the steps. It was too late.

Now a man appeared in the entrance, his hands in his pockets. He wore a dark, untidy coat, and a cap pulled down over his forehead. The man glanced at her and said something to her.

At once Barris strode up the steps after her. He took her by the arm, stepping between her and the man. "Watch it," he said to the man, putting his hand on the pencil beam which he carried in his breast pocket.

In a slow, quiet voice the man said, "Don't get excited, mister." He studied Barris. "I wasn't accosting Mrs. Pitt. I was merely asking when you arrived." Coming around behind Barris and

Rachel, he said, "Go on inside the hotel, Director. We have a room upstairs where we can talk. No one will bother us here. You picked a good place."

Or rather, Barris thought icily, the cab and Rachel Pitt picked a good place. There was nothing he could do; he felt, against his spine, the tip of the man's heat beam.

"You shouldn't be suspicious of a man of the cloth, in regards to such matters," the man said conversationally, as they crossed the grimy, dark lobby to the stairs. The elevator, Barris noticed, was out of order; or at least it was so labeled. "Or perhaps," the man said, "you failed to notice the historic badge of my vocation." At the stairs the man halted, glanced around, and removed his cap.

The stern, heavy-browed face that became visible was familiar to Barris. The slightly crooked nose, as if it had been broken once and never properly set. The deliberately short-cropped hair that gave the man's entire face the air of grim austerity.

Rachel said, "This is Father Fields."

The man smiled, and Barris saw irregular, massive teeth. The photo had not indicated that, Barris thought. Nor the strong chin. It had hinted at, but not really given, the full measure of the man. In some ways Father Fields looked more like a toughened, weathered prize fighter than he did a man of religion.

Barris, face to face with him for the first time, felt a complete and absolute fear of the man; it came with a certitude that he had never before known in his life.

Ahead of them, Rachel led the way upstairs.

# CHAPTER EIGHT

Barris said, "I'd be interested to know when this woman went over to you." He indicated Rachel Pitt, who stood by a window of the hotel room, gazing meditatively out at the buildings and rooftops of Geneva.

"You can see Unity Control from here," Rachel said, turning her head.

"Of course you can," Father Fields said in his hoarse, grumbling voice. He sat in the corner, in a striped bathrobe and fleece-lined slippers, a screw driver in one hand, a light fixture in the other; he had gone into the bathroom to take a shower, but the light wasn't working. Two other men, Healers evidently, sat at a card table poring over some pamphlets stacked up between them in wired bundles. Barris assumed that these were propaganda material of the Movement, about to be distributed.

"Is that just coincidence?" Rachel asked.

Fields grunted, ignoring her as he worked on the light fixture. Then, raising his head, he said brusquely to Barris, "Now listen. I won't lie to you, because it's lies that your organization is founded on. Anyone who knows me knows I never have need of lying. Why should I? The truth is my greatest weapon."

"What is the truth?" Barris said.

"The truth is that pretty soon we're going to run up that street you see outside to that big building the lady is looking at, and then Unity won't exist." He smiled, showing his malformed teeth. But it was, oddly, a friendly smile. As if, Barris thought, the man hoped that he would chime in—possibly smile back in agreement.

With massive irony, Barris said, "Good luck."

"Luck," Fields echoed. "We don't need it. All we need is speed. It'll be like poking at some old rotten fruit with a stick." His voice twanged with a regional accent of his origin; Barris caught the drawl of Taubmann's territory, the Southern States that formed the rim of South America.

"Spare me your folksy metaphors," Barris said.

Fields laughed. "You stand in error, Mister Director."

"It was a simile," Rachel agreed, expressionlessly.

Barris felt himself redden; they were making fun of him, these people, and he was falling into it. He said to the man in the striped bathrobe, "I'm amazed at your power to draw followers. You engineer the murder of this woman's husband, and after meeting you she joins your Movement. That is impressive."

For a time Fields said nothing. Finally he threw down the light fixture. "Must be a hundred years old," he said. "Nothing like that in the United States since I was born. And they call this area 'modern.'" He scowled and plucked at his lower lip. "I appreciate your moral indignation. Somebody did smash in that poor man's head; there's no doubt about that."

"You were there too," Barris said.

"Oh, yes," Fields said. He studied Barris intently; the hard dark eyes seemed to grow and become even more wrathful. "I do get carried away," he said. "When I see that lovely little suit you people wear, that gray suit and white shirt, those shiny black shoes." His scrutiny traveled up and down Barris. "And especially, I get carried away by that thing you all have in your pockets. Those pencil beams."

Rachel said to Barris, "Father Fields was once burned by a tax collector."

"Yes," Fields said. "You know your Unity tax collectors are

exempt from the law. No citizen can take legal action against them. Isn't that lovely?" Lifting his arm, he pulled back his right sleeve; Barris saw that the flesh had been corroded away to a permanent mass of scar tissue, from the man's wrist to his elbow. "Let's see some moral indignation about that," he said to Barris.

"I have it," Barris said. "I never approved of the general tax-collecting procedures. You won't find them in my area."

"That's so," Fields said. His voice lost some of its ferocity; he seemed to cool slightly. "That's a fact about you. Compared to the other Directors, you're not too bad. We have a couple of people in and around your offices. We know quite a bit about you. You're here in Geneva because you want to find out why Vulcan 3 hasn't handed down any dogma about us Healers. It needles your conscience that old Jason Dill can toss your DQ forms back in your face and there's nothing you can do. It is mighty odd that your machine hasn't said anything about us."

To that, Barris said nothing.

"It gives us sort of an advantage," Fields said. "You boys don't have any operating policy; you have to mark time until the machine talks. Because it wouldn't occur to you to put together your own human-made policy."

Barris said, "In my area I have a policy. I have as many Healers as possible thrown into jail—on sight."

"Why?" Rachel Pitt asked.

"Ask your dead husband," Barris said, with animosity toward her. "I can't understand you," he said to her. "Your husband went out on his job and these people—"

Fields interrupted, "Director, you have never been worked over by the Atlanta psychologists." His voice was quiet. "This woman has. So was I, to some extent. To a very minor extent. Not like she was. With her, they were in a hurry."

For a while no one spoke.

There's not much I can say, Barris realized. He walked over to the card table and picked up one of the pamphlets; aimlessly, he read the large black type.

DO YOU HAVE ANY SAY IN RUNNING YOUR LIVES?
WHEN WAS THE LAST TIME YOU VOTED?

"There has been no public election," Fields said, "for twenty years. Do they teach that to the little kids in your schools?"

"There should be," Barris said.

Fields said, "Mr. Barris—" His voice was tense and husky. "How'd you like to be the first Director to come over to us?" For an instant Barris detected a pleading quality; then it was gone. The man's voice and face became stern. "It'll make you look good as hell in the future history books," he said, and laughed harshly. Then, once more picking up the light fixture, he resumed work on it. He ignored Barris; he did not even seem to be waiting for a reply.

Coming over to Barris, Rachel said in her sharp, constricted fashion, "Director, he's not joking. He really wants you to join the Movement."

"I imagine he does," Barris said.

Fields said, "You have a sense of what's wrong. You know how wrong it is. All that ambition and suspicion. What's it for? Maybe I'm doing you people an injustice, but honest to God, Mr. Barris, I think your top men are insane. I know Jason Dill is. Most of the Directors are, and their staffs. And the schools are turning out lunatics. Did you know they took my daughter and stuck her into one of their schools? As far as I know she's there now. We never got into the schools too well. You people are really strong, there. It means a lot to you."

"You went to a Unity school," Rachel said to Barris. "You know how they teach children not to question, not to disagree. They're taught to obey. Arthur was the product of one of them. Pleasant, good-looking, well-dressed, on his way up—" She broke off.

And dead, Barris thought.

"If you don't join us," Fields said to him, "you can walk out the door and up the street to your appointment with Jason Dill."

"I have no appointment," Barris said.

"That's right," Fields admitted.

Rachel screamed, pointing to the window.

Coming across the sill, through the window and into the room, was something made of gleaming metal. It lifted and flew through the air. As it swooped it made a shrill sound. It changed direction and dropped at Fields.

The two men at the card table leaped up and stared open-mouthed. One of them began groping for the gun at his waist.

The metal thing dived at Fields. Covering his face with his arms, Fields flung himself to the floor and rolled. His striped bathrobe flapped, and one slipper shot from his foot and slid across the rug. As he rolled and grabbed out a heat beam and fired upward, sweeping the air above him. A burning flash seared Barris; he leaped back and shut his eyes.

Still screaming, Rachel Pitt appeared in front of him, her face torn with hysteria. The air crackled with energy; a cloud of dense blue-gray matter obscured most of the room. The couch, the chairs, the rug and walls were burning. Smoke poured up, and Barris saw tongues of flame winking orange in the murk. Now he heard Rachel choke; her screams ceased. He himself was partly blinded. He made his way toward the door, his ears ringing.

"It's okay," Father Fields said, his voice coming dimly through the crackling of energy. "Get those little fires out. I got the god-damn thing." He loomed up in front of Barris, grinning crookedly. One side of his face was badly burned and part of his short-cropped hair had been seared away. His scalp, red and blistered, seemed to glow. "If you can help get the fires out," he said to Barris in an almost courtly tone, "maybe I can find enough of the goddamn thing to get into it and see what it was."

One of the men had found a hand-operated fire extinguisher outside in the hall; now, pumping furiously, he was managing to get the fires out. His companion appeared with another extin-guisher and pitched in. Barris left them to handle the fire and went back through the room to find Rachel Pitt.

She was crouched in the far corner, sunk down in a heap, staring straight ahead, her hands clasped together. When he lifted her up, he felt her body trembling. She said nothing as he stood holding her in his arms; she did not seem aware of him.

Appearing beside him, Fields said in a gleeful voice, "Hot dog, Barris—I found most of it." He triumphantly displayed a charred but still intact metal cylinder with an elaborate system of antennas and receptors and propulsion jets. Then, seeing Rachel Pitt, he lost his smile. "I wonder if she'll come out of it this time," he said. "She was this way when she first came to us. After the Atlanta boys let her go. It's catatonia."

"And you got her out of it?" Barris said.

Fields said, "She came out of it because she wanted to. She wanted to do something. Be active. Help us. Maybe this blast was too much for her. She's stood a lot." He shrugged, but his face was an expression of great compassion.

"Maybe I'll see you again," Barris said to him.

"You're leaving?" Fields said. "Where are you going?"

"To see Jason Dill."

"What about her?" Fields said, indicating the woman in Barris' arms. "Are you taking her with you?"

"If you'll let me," Barris said.

"Do what you want," Fields said, eyeing him thoughtfully. "I don't quite understand you, Director." He seemed, in this moment, to have shed his regional accent. "Are you for us or against us? Or do you know? Maybe you don't know; maybe it'll take time."

Barris said, "I'll never go along with a group that murders."

"There are slow murders and fast murders," Fields said. "And body murders and mind murders. Some you do with evil schools."

Going past him, Barris went on out of the smoke-saturated room, into the hall outside. He descended the stairs to the lobby.

Outside on the sidewalk he hailed a robot cab.


At the Geneva field he put Mrs. Pitt aboard a ship that would carry her to his own region, North America. He contacted his staff by vidsender and gave them instructions to have the ship met when it landed in New York and to provide her with medical care until he himself got back. And he had one final order for them.

"Don't let her out of my jurisdiction. Don't honor any request to have her transferred, especially to South America."

The staff member said acutely, "You don't want to let this person get anywhere near Atlanta."

"That's right," Barris said, aware that without his having to spell it out his staff understood the situation. There was probably no one in the Unity structure who would not be able to follow his meaning. Atlanta was the prime object of dread for all of them, great and small alike.

Does Jason Dill have that hanging over him too? Barris wondered as he left the vidbooth. Possibly he is exempt—certainly from a rational viewpoint he has nothing to fear. But the irrational fear could be there anyhow.

He made his way through the crowded, noisy terminal building, headed in the direction of one of the lunch counters. At the counter he ordered a sandwich and coffee and sat with that for a time, pulling himself together and pondering.

Was there really a letter to Dill accusing me of treason? he asked himself. Had Rachel been telling the truth? Probably not. It probably had been a device to draw him aside, to keep him from going on to Unity Control.

I'll have to take the chance, he decided. No doubt I could put out careful feelers, track the information down over a period of time; I might even know within a week. But I can't wait that long. I want to face Dill now. That's what I came here for.

He thought, And I have been with them, the enemy. If such a letter exists, there is now what would no doubt be called "proof." The structure would need nothing more; I would be tried for treason and convicted. And that would be the end of me, as a high official of the system and as a living, breathing human being. True, something might still be walking around, but it wouldn't really be alive.

And yet, he realized, I can't even go back now, to my own region. Whether I like it or not I have met Father Fields face-to-face; I've associated with him, and any enemies I might have, inside or outside the Unity structure, will have exactly what they want—for the rest of my life. It's too late to give up, to drop the idea of confronting Jason Dill. With irony, he thought, Father Fields has forced me to go through with it, the thing he was trying to prevent.

He paid for his lunch and left the lunch counter. Going outside onto the sidewalk, he called another robot cab and instructed it to take him to Unity Control.

Barris pushed past the battery of secretaries and clerks, into Jason Dill's private syndrome of interconnected offices. At the sight of his Director's stripe, the dark red slash on his gray coatsleeve, officials of the Unity Control stepped obediently out of his path, leaving a way open from room to room. The last door opened—and abruptly he was facing Dill.

Jason Dill looked up slowly, putting down a handful of reports. "What do you think you're doing?" He did not appear at first to recognize Barris; his gaze strayed to the Director's stripe and then back to his face. "This is out of the question," Dill said, "your barging in here like this."

"I came here to talk to you," Barris said. He shut the office door after him; it closed with a bang, startling the older man. Jason Dill half stood up, then subsided.

"Director Barris," he murmured. His eyes narrowed. "File a regular appointment slip; you know procedure well enough by now to—"

Barris cut him off. "Why did you turn back my DQ form? Are you withholding information from Vulcan 3?"

Silence.

The color left Jason Dill's face. "Your form wasn't properly filled out. According to Section Six, Article Ten of the Unity—"

"You're rerouting material away from Vulcan 3; that's why it hasn't stated a policy on the Healers." He came closer to the seated man, bending over him as Dill stared down at his papers on the desk, not meeting his gaze. "Why? It doesn't make sense.

You know what this constitutes. Treason! Keeping back data, deliberately falsifying the troughs. I could bring charges against you, even have you arrested." Resting his hands on the surface of the desk, Barris said loudly, "Is the purpose of this to isolate and weaken the eleven Directors so that—"

He broke off. He was looking down into the barrel of a pencil beam. Jason Dill had been holding it since he had burst into the man's office. Dill's middle-aged features twitched bleakly; his eyes gleamed as he gripped the small tube. "Now be quiet, Director," Dill said icily. "I admire your tactics. This going on the offensive. Accusations without opportunity for me even to get in one word. Standard operating procedure." He breathed slowly, in a series of great gasps. "Damn you," he snapped, *"sit down."*

Barris sat down watchfully. I made my pitch, he realized. The man is right. And shrewd. He's seen a lot in his time, more than I have. Maybe I'm not the first to barge in here, yelling with indignation, trying to pin him down, force admissions.

Thinking that, Barris felt his confidence ebb away. But he continued to face the older man; he did not draw back.

Jason Dill's face was gray now. Drops of perspiration stood out on his wrinkled forehead; bringing out his handkerchief he patted at them. With the other hand, however, he still held the pencil beam. "We're both a little calmer," he said. "Which in my opinion is better. You were overly dramatic. Why?" A faint, distorted smile appeared on his lips. "Have you been practicing how you would make your entrance?"

The man's hand traveled to his breast pocket. He rubbed a bulge there; Barris saw that he had something in his inner pocket, something to which his hand had gone involuntarily. Seeing what he had done, Dill at once jerked his hand away.

Medicine? Barris wondered.

"This treason gambit," Dill said. "I could try that, too. An attempted coup on your part." He pointed at a control on the edge of his desk. "All this—your grand entrance—has of course been recorded. The evidence is there." He pressed a stud, and, on the desk vidscreen, the Geneva Unity monitor appeared. "Give me the police," Dill said. Sitting with the pencil beam still pointed at Barris, he waited for the line to be put through. "I have too many other problems to take time off to cope with a Director who decides to run amuck."

Barris said, "I'll fight this all the way in the Unity courts. My conscience is clear; I'm acting in the interests of Unity, against a Managing Director who's systematically breaking down the system, step by step. You can investigate my entire life and you won't find a thing. I know I'll beat you in the courts, even if it takes years."

"We have a letter," Dill said. On the screen the familiar heavy-jowled features of a police official appeared. "Stand by," Dill instructed him. The police official's eyes moved as he took in the scene of the Managing Director holding his gun on Director Barris.

"That letter," Barris said as steadily as possible, "has no factual basis for the charges it makes."

"Oh?" Dill said. "You're familiar with its charges?"

"Rachel Pitt gave me all the information," Barris said. So she had been telling the truth. Well, that letter—spurious as its charges were—coupled with this episode, would probably be enough to convict him. The two would dovetail; they would create together the sort of evidence acceptable to the Unity mentality.

The police official eyed Barris.

At his desk, Jason Dill held the pencil beam steadily.

Barris said, "Today I sat in the same room with Father Fields."

Reaching his hand out to the vidsender, Jason Dill reflected and then said, "I'll ring you off and recontact you later." With his thumb he broke the connection; the image of the police official, still staring at Barris, faded out.

Jason Dill rose from his desk and pulled loose the power cable supplying the recording scanner which had been on since Barris entered the room. Then he reseated himself.

"The charges in the letter are true!" he said with incredulity. "My God, it never occurred to me . . . " Then, rubbing his forehead he said, "Yes, it did. Briefly. So they managed to penetrate to the Director level." His eyes showed horror and weariness.

"They put a gun on me and detained me," Barris said. "When I got here to Geneva."

Doubt, mixed with distraught cunning, crossed the older man's face. Obviously, he did not want to believe that the Healers had gotten so far up into Unity, Barris realized. He would grasp at any straw, any explanation which would account for the facts . . . even the true one, Barris thought bitingly. Jason Dill had a psychological need that took precedence over the habitual organizational suspicions.

"You can trust me," Barris said.

"Why?" The pencil beam still pointed at him, but the conflicting emotions swept back and forth through the man.

"You have to believe someone," Barris said. "Sometime, somewhere. What is that you reach up and rub, there at your chest?"

Grimacing, Dill glanced down at his hand; again it was at his chest. He jerked it away. "Don't play on my fears," he said.

"Your fear of isolation?" Barris said. "Of having everyone against you? Is that some physical injury that you keep rubbing?"

Dill said, "No. You're guessing far too much; you're out of your depth." But he seemed more composed now. "Well, Director," he said. "I'll tell you something. I probably don't have long to live. My health has deteriorated since I've had this job. Maybe in a sense you're right . . . it *is* a physical injury I'm rubbing. If you ever get where I am, you'll have some deep-seated injuries and illnesses too. Because there'll be people around you putting them there."

"Maybe you should take a couple of flying wedge squads of police and seize the Bond Hotel," Barris said. "He was there an hour ago. Down in the old section of the city. Not more than two miles from here."

"He'd be gone," Dill said. "He turns up again and again on the outskirts this way. We'll never get him; there're a million ratholes he can slither down."

Barris said, "You almost did get him."

"When?"

"In the hotel room. When that robot tracking device entered and made for him. It almost succeeded in burning him up, but he was quite fast; he managed to roll away and get it first."

Dill said, "What robot tracking device? Describe it." As Barris described it, Dill stared at him starkly. He swallowed noisily but did not interrupt until Barris had finished.

"What's wrong?" Barris said. "From what I saw of it, it seems to be the most effective counterpenetration weapon you have. Surely you'll be able to break up the Movement with such a mechanism. I think your anxiety and preoccupation is excessive."

In an almost inaudible voice, Dill said, "Agnes Parker."

"Who is that?" Barris said.

Seemingly not aware of him, Dill murmured, "Vulcan 2. And now a try at Father Fields. But he got away." Putting down his pencil beam he reached into his coat; rummaging, he brought out two reels of tape. He tossed the tape down on the desk.

"So that's what you've been carrying," Barris said with curiosity. He picked up the reels and examined them.

Dill said, "Director, there is a third force."

"What?" Barris said, with a chill.

"A third force is operating on us," Jason Dill said, and smiled grotesquely. "It may get all of us. It appears to be very strong."

He put his pencil beam away, then. The two of them faced each other without it.

# CHAPTER NINE

The police raid on the Bond Hotel, although carried out expertly and thoroughly, netted nothing.

Jason Dill was not surprised.

In his office by himself he faced a legal dictation machine. Clearing his throat he said into it hurriedly, "This is to act as a formal statement in the event of my death, explaining the circumstances and reasons why I saw fit as Unity Managing Director to conduct *sub rosa* relations with North American Director William Barris. I entered into these relations knowing full well that Director Barris was under heavy suspicion concerning his position vis-à-vis the Healers' Movement, a treasonable band of murderers and—" He could not think of the word so he cut off the machine temporarily.

He glanced at his watch. In five minutes he had an appointment with Barris; he would not have time to complete his protective statement anyway. So he erased the tape. Better to start over later on, he decided. If he survived into the later on.

I'll go meet him, Jason Dill decided, and go on the assumption that he is being honest with me. I'll cooperate with him fully; I'll hold nothing back.

But just to be on the safe side, he opened the drawer of his desk and lifted out a small container. From it he took an object wrapped up and sealed; he opened it, and there was the smallest heat beam that the police had been able to manufacture. No larger than a kidney bean.

Using the adhesive agent provided, he carefully affixed the weapon inside his right ear. Its color blended with his own; examining himself in a wall mirror he felt satisfied that the heat beam would not be noticed.

Now he was ready for his appointment. Taking his overcoat, he left his office, walking briskly.

He stood by while Barris laid the tapes out on the surface of a table, spreading them flat with his hands.

"And no more came after these," Barris said.

"No more," Dill said. "Vulcan 2 ceased to exist at that point." He indicated the first of the two tapes. "Start reading there."

*This Movement may be of more significance than first appears. It is evident that the Movement is directed against Vulcan 3 rather than the series of computers as a whole. Until I have had time to consider the greater aspects, I suggest Vulcan 3 not be informed of the matter.*

"I asked why," Dill said. "Look at the next tape."

*Consider the basic difference between Vulcan 3 and preceding computer. Its decisions are more than strictly factual evaluations of objective data; essentially it is creating policy at a value level. Vulcan 3 deals with teleological problems . . . the significance of this cannot be immediately inferred. I must consider it at greater length.*

"And that's it," Dill said. "The end. Presumably Vulcan 2 did consider it at greater length. Anyhow, it's a metaphysical problem; we'll never know either way."

"These tapes look old," Barris said. Examining the first one he said, "This is older than the other. By some months."

Jason Dill said, "The first tape is fifteen months old. The second—" He shrugged. "Four or five. I forget."

"This first tape was put out by Vulcan 2 over a year ago," Barris said, "and from that time on, Vulcan 3 gave out no directives concerning the Healers."

Dill nodded.

"You followed Vulcan 2's advice," Barris said. "From the moment you read this tape you ceased informing Vulcan 3 about the growth of the Movement." Studying the older man he said, "You've been withholding information from Vulcan 3 *without knowing why.*" The disbelief on his face grew; his lips twisted with outrage. "And all these months, all this time, you went on carrying out what Vulcan 2 told you to do! Good God, *which is the machine and which is the man?* And you clasp these two reels of tape to your bosom—" Unable to go on, Barris clamped his jaws shut, his eyes furious with accusation.

Feeling his own face redden, Dill said, "You must understand the relationship that existed between me and Vulcan 2. We had always worked together, back in the old days. Vulcan 2 was limited, of course, compared with Vulcan 3; it was obsolete—it couldn't have held the authoritative position Vulcan 3 now holds, determining ultimate policy. All it could do was assist . . ." He heard his voice trail off miserably. And then resentment clouded up inside him; here he was, defending himself guiltily to his inferior officer. This was absurd!

Barris said, "Once a bureaucrat, always a bureaucrat. No matter how highly placed." His voice had an icy, deadly quality; in it there was no compassion for the older man. Dill felt his flesh wince at the impact. He turned, then, and walked away, his back to Barris. Not facing him, he said:

"I admit I was partial to Vulcan 2. Perhaps I did tend to trust it too much."

"So you did find something you could trust. Maybe the Healers are right. About all of us."

"You detest me because I put my faith in a machine? My God, every time you read a gauge or a dial or a meter, every time you ride in a car or a ship, aren't you putting your faith in a machine?"

Barris nodded reluctantly. "But it's not the same," he said.

"You don't know," Dill said. "You never had my job. There's no difference between my faith in what these tapes tell me to do, and the faith the water-meter reader has when he reads the meter and writes down the reading. Vulcan 3 was dangerous and Vulcan 2 knew it. Am I supposed to cringe with shame because I shared Vulcan 2's intuition? I felt the same thing, the first time I watched those goddamn letters flowing across that surface."

"Would you be willing to let me look at the remains of Vulcan 2?" Barris said.

"It could be arranged," Dill said. "All we need are papers that certify you as a maintenance repairman with top clearance. I would advise you not to wear your Director's stripe, in that case."

"Fine," Barris said. "Let's get started on that, then."

At the entrance of the gloomy, deserted chamber, he stood gazing at the heaps of ruin that had been the old computer. The silent metal and twisted parts, fused together in a useless, shapeless mass. Too bad to see it like this, he thought, and never to have seen it the way it was. Or maybe not. Beside him, Jason Dill seemed overcome; his body slumped and he scratched compulsively at his right ear, evidently barely aware of the man whom he had brought.

Barris said, "Not much left."

"They knew what they were doing." Dill spoke almost to himself; then, with great effort, he roused himself. "I heard one of them in the corridor. I even saw it. The eyes gleaming. It was hanging around. I thought it was only a bat or an owl. I went on out."

Squatting down, Barris picked up a handful of smashed wiring and relays. "Has an attempt been made to reconstruct any of this?"

"Vulcan 2?" Dill murmured. "As I've said, destruction was so complete and on such a scale—"

"The *components*," Barris said. He lifted a complex plastic tube carefully. "This, for instance. This wheeling valve. The envelope is gone, of course, but the elements look intact."

Dill eyed him doubtfully. "You're advancing the idea that there might be parts of it still alive?"

"Mechanically intact," Barris said. "Portions which can be made to function within some other frame. It seems to me we can't really proceed until we can establish what Vulcan 2 had determined about Vulcan 3. We can make good guesses on our own, but that might not be the same."

"I'll have a repair crew make a survey on the basis which you propose," Dill said. "We'll see what can be done. It would take time, of course. What do you suggest in the meanwhile? In your opinion, should I continue the policy already laid down?"

Barris said, "Feed Vulcan 3 some data that you've been holding back. I'd like to see its reaction to a couple of pieces of news."

"Such as?"

"The news about Vulcan 2's destruction."

Floundering, Dill said, "That would be too risky. We're not sure enough of our ground. Suppose we were wrong."

I doubt if we are, Barris thought. There seems less doubt of it all time. But maybe we should at least wait until we've tried to rebuild the destroyed computer. "There's a good deal of risk," he said aloud. "To us, to Unity." To everyone, he realized.

Nodding, Jason Dill again reached up and plucked at his ear.

"What do you have there?" Barris said. Now that the man had stopped carrying his two tape-reels he had evidently found something else to fall back on, some replacement symbol of security.

"N-nothing," Dill stammered, flushing. "A nervous tic, I suppose. From the tension." He held out his hand. "Give me those parts you picked up. We'll need them for the reconstruction. I'll see that you're notified as soon as there's anything to look at."

"No," Barris said. He decided on the spot, and, having done so, pushed on with as much force as he could muster. "I'd prefer not to have the work done here. I want it done in North America."

Dill stared at him in bewilderment. Then, gradually, his face darkened. "In your region. By your crews."

"That's right," Barris said. "What you've told me may all be a fraud. These reels of tape could easily be fakes. All I can be sure of is this: my original notion about you is correct, the notion that brought me here." He made his voice unyielding, without any doubt in it. "Your withholding of information from Vulcan 3 constitutes a crime against Unity. I'd be willing to fight you in the Unity courts any time, as an act of duty on my part. Possibly the rationalizations you've given are true, but until I can get some verification from these bits and pieces . . . " He swept up a handful of relays, switches, wiring.

For a long, long time Dill was silent. He stood, as before, with his hand pressed against his right ear. Then at last he sighed. "Okay, Director. I'm just too tired to fight with you. Take the stuff. Bring your crew in here and load it, if you want; cart it out and take it to New York. Play around with it until you're satisfied." Turning, he walked away, out of the chamber and up the dim, echoing corridor.

Barris, his hands full of the pieces of Vulcan 2, watched him go. When the man had disappeared out of sight, Barris once more began to breathe. It's over, he realized. I've won. There won't be any charge against me; I came to Geneva and confronted him—and I got away with it.

His hands shaking with relief, he began sorting among the ruins, taking his time, beginning a thorough, methodical job.

By eight o'clock the next morning the remains of Vulcan 2 had been crated and loaded onto a commercial transport. By eight-thirty Barris' engineers had been able to get the last of the original wiring diagrams pertaining to Vulcan 2. And at nine, when transport finally took off for New York, Barris breathed a sigh of relief. Once the ship was off the ground, Jason Dill ceased to have authority over it.

Barris himself followed in the ten o'clock passenger flight, the swift little luxurious ship provided for tourists and business-men traveling between New York and Geneva. It gave him a chance to bathe and shave and change his clothes; he had been hard at work all night.

In the first-class lounge he relaxed in one of the deep chairs, enjoying himself for the first time in weeks. The buzz of voices around him lulled him into a semidoze; he lay back, passively watching the smartly dressed women going up the aisles, listening to snatches of conversation, mostly social, going on around him.

"A drink, sir?" the robot attendant asked, coming up by him.

He ordered a good dark German beer and with it the cheese hors d'oeuvres for which the flight was famous.

While he sat eating a wedge of *port de salut,* he caught sight of the headlines of the *London Times* which the man across from him was reading. At once he was on his feet, searching for the newspaper-vending robot; he found it, bought his own copy of the paper, and hurried back to his seat.

DIRECTORS TAUBMANN AND HENDERSON
CHARGE AUTHORITY IN ILLINOIS HEALERS
VICTORY. DEMAND INVESTIGATION

Stunned, he read on to discover that a carefully planned mass uprising of the Movement in Illinois rural towns had been co-ordinated with a revolt of the Chicago working class; together, the two groups had put an end—at least temporarily—to Unity control of most of the state.

One further item, very small, also chilled him.

NORTH AMERICAN DIRECTOR BARRIS UN-
AVAILABLE. NOT IN NEW YORK

They had been active during his absence; they had made good use of it. And not just the Movement, he realized grimly. Taubmann, also. And Henderson, the Director of Asia Minor. The two had teamed up more than once in the past.

The investigation, of course, would be a function of Jason Dill's office. Barris thought, I barely managed to handle Dill before this; all he needs is a little support from Taubmann, and the ground will be cut from under my feet. Even now, while I'm stuck here in mid-flight . . . Possibly Dill himself instigated this; they may already have joined forces, Dill and Taubmann— ganging up on me.

His mind spun on, and then he managed to get hold of himself. I am in a good position, he decided. I have the remains of Vulcan 2 in my possession, and, most important of all, I forced Dill to admit to me what he has been doing. *No one else knows!* He would never dare take action against me, now that I have that knowledge. If I made it public . . .

I still hold the winning hand, he decided. In spite of this cleverly timed demand for an investigation of my handling of the Movement in my area.

That damn Fields, he thought. Sitting there in the hotel room, complimenting me as the "one decent Director," and then doing his best to discredit me while I was away from my region.

Hailing one of the robot attendants, he ordered, "Bring me a vidsender. One on a closed-circuit line to New York Unity."

He had the soundproof curtains of his chair drawn, and a few moments later he was facing the image of his sub-Director, Peter Allison, on the vidscreen.

"I wouldn't be alarmed," Allison said, after Barris had made his concern clear. "This Illinois uprising is being put down by our police crews. And in addition it's part of a worldwide pattern.

They seem to be active almost everywhere, now. When you get back here I'll show you the classified reports; most of the Directors have been keeping the activity out of the newspapers. If it weren't for Taubmann and Henderson, this business in Illinois might have been kept quiet. As I get it, there've been similar strikes in Lisbon and Berlin and Stalingrad. If we could get some kind of decision from Vulcan 3—"

"Maybe we will, fairly soon," Barris said.

"You made out satisfactorily in Geneva? You're coming back with definite word from it?"

"I'll discuss it with you later," Barris said, and broke the connection.

Later, as the ship flew low over New York, he saw the familiar signs of hyperactivity there, too. A procession of brown-clad Healers moved along a side street in the Bowery, solemn and dignified in their coarse garments. Crowds watched in respectful admiration. There was a demolished Unity auto—destroyed by a mob, not more than a mile from his offices. When the ship began its landing maneuver, he managed to catch sight of chalked slogans on building walls. Posters. So much more in the open, he realized. Blatant. They had progressively less to fear.

He had beaten the commercial transport carrying the remains of Vulcan 2 by almost an hour. After he had checked in at his offices and signed the formal papers regaining administrative authority from Allison, he asked about Rachel.

Allison said, "You're referring to the widow of that Unity man slain in South America?" Leafing through an armload of papers and reports and forms, the man at last came up with one. "So much has been going on since you were last here," he explained. "It seems as if everything broke over us at once." He turned a page. "Here it is. Mrs. Arthur Pitt arrived here yesterday at 2:30 A.M. New York time and was signed over to us by the personnel responsible for her safe transit from Europe. We then arranged to have her taken at once to the mental health institute in Denver."

Human lives, Barris thought. Marks on forms.

"I think I'll go to Denver," he said. "For a few hours. A big transport will be coming in here from Unity Control any time now; make sure it's fully guarded at all times and don't let anyone pry into it or start uncrating the stuff inside. I want to be present during most of the process."

"Shall I continue to deal with the Illinois situation?" Allison asked, following after him. "It's my impression that I've been relatively successful there; if you have time to examine the—"

Barris said, "You keep on with that. But keep me informed."

Ten minutes later he was aboard a small emergency ship that belonged to his office, speeding across the United States toward Colorado. I wonder if she will be there, he asked himself. He had a fatalistic dread. They'll have sent her on. Probably to New Mexico, to some health farm there. And when I get there, they'll have transferred her to New Orleans, the rim-city of Taubmann's domain. And from there, an easy, effortless bureaucratic step to Atlanta.

But at the Denver hospital the doctor who met him said, "Yes, Director. We have Mrs. Pitt with us. At present she's out on the solarium." He pointed that way. "Taking things easy," the doctor said, accompanying him part way. "She's responded quite well to our techniques. I think she'll be up and on her feet, back to normal, in a few days."

Out on the glass-walled balcony, Barris found her. She was lying curled up on a redwood lawn bench, her knees pulled up tightly against her, her arms wrapped around her calves, her head resting to one side. She wore a short blue outfit which he recognized as hospital convalescent issue. Her feet were bare.

"Looks like you're getting along fine," he said awkwardly.

For a time she said nothing. Then she stirred and said, "Hi. When did you get here?"

"Just now," he said, regarding her with apprehension; he felt himself stiffen. Something was still wrong.

Rachel said, "Look over there." She pointed, and he saw a plastic shipping carton lying open, its top off. "It was addressed to both of us," she said, "but they gave it to me. Someone put it on the ship at a stop somewhere. Probably one of those men who clean up. A lot of them are Healers."

Grabbing at the carton, he saw inside it the charred metal cylinder, the half-destroyed gleaming eyes. As he gazed down he saw the eyes respond; they recorded his presence.

"He repaired it," Rachel said in a flat, emotionless voice. "I've been sitting here listening to it."

"*Listening* to it?"

"It talks," Rachel said. "That's all it does; that's all he could fix. It never stops talking. But I can't understand anything it says. You try. It isn't talking to us." She added, "Father fixed it so it isn't harmful. It won't go anywhere or do anything."

Now he heard it. A high-pitched blearing, constant and yet altering each second. A continual signal emitted by the thing. And Rachel was right. It was not directed at them.

"Father thought you would know what it is," she said. "There's a note with it. He says he can't figure it out. He can't figure out who it's talking to." She picked up a piece of paper and held it out. Curiously, she said, "Do you know who it's talking to?"

"Yes," Barris said, staring down at the crippled, blighted metal thing deliberately imprisoned in its carton; Father Fields had taken care to hobble it thoroughly. "I guess I do."

# CHAPTER TEN

The leader of the New York repair crew contacted Barris early the following month. "First report on reconstruction work, Director," Smith reported.

"Any results?" Neither Barris nor his chief repairman uttered the name Vulcan 2 aloud; this was a closed-circuit vidchannel they were using, but with the burgeoning of the Healers' Movement absolute secrecy had to be maintained in every area. Already, a number of infiltrators had been exposed, and several of them had been employed in the communications media. The vidservice was a natural place. All Unity business sooner or later was put over the lines.

Smith said, "Not much yet. Most of the components were beyond salvage. Only a fraction of the memory store still exists intact."

Becoming tense, Barris said, "Find anything relevant?"

On the vidscreen, Smith's sweat-streaked, grimy face was expressionless. "A few things, I think. If you want to drop over, we'll show you what we've done."

As soon as he could wind up pressing business, Barris drove across New York to the Unity work labs. He was checked by the guards and passed through into the restricted inner area, the functioning portion of the labs. There he found Wade Smith and his subordinates standing around a complex tangle of pulsing machinery.

"There it is," Smith said.

"Looks different," Barris said. He saw in it almost nothing familiar; all the visible parts appeared to be new, not from the old computer.

"We've done our best to activate the undamaged elements." With obvious pride, Smith indicated a particularly elaborate mass of gleaming wiring, dials, meters, and power cables. "The wheeling valves are now scanned directly, without reference to any overall structure, and the impulses are sorted and fed into an audio system. Scanning has to be virtually at random, under such adverse circumstances. We've done all we can to unscramble—especially to get out the noise. Remember, the computer maintained its own organizing principle, which is gone, of course. We have to take the surviving memory digits as they come."

Smith clicked on the largest of the wall-mounted speakers. A hoarse roar filled the room, an indistinguishable blur of static and sound. He adjusted several of the control settings.

"Hard to make out," Barris said, after straining in vain.

"Impossible at first. It takes a while. After you've listened to it as much as we have—"

Barris nodded in disappointment. "I thought maybe we'd wind up with better results. But I know you did everything possible."

"We're working on a wholly new sorting mechanism. Given three or four more weeks, we'll possibly have something far superior to this."

"Too long," Barris said instantly. Far too long. The uprising at Chicago, far from being reversed by Unity police, had spread into adjoining states and was now nearing a union with a similar Movement action in the area around St. Louis. "In four weeks," he said to the repairmen gathered around, "we'll probably be wearing coarse brown robes. And instead of trying to patch up this stuff"— he indicated the vast gleaming structure containing the extant elements of Vulcan 2—"we'll more likely be tearing it down."

It was a grim joke, and none of the repairmen smiled. Barris said, "I'd like to listen to this noise." He indicated the roar from the wall speaker. "Why don't you all clear out for a little while, so I can see what I can pick up."

At that point Smith and his crew departed. Barris took up a position in front of the speaker and prepared himself for a long session.

Somewhere, lost in the fog of random and meaningless sound, were faint traces of words. Computations—the vague unwinding of the memory elements as the newly constructed scanner moved over the old remains. Barris clasped his hands together, tensing himself in an effort to hear.

" . . . *progressive bifurcation* . . ."

One phrase; he had picked out something, small as it was, one jot from the chaos.

" . . . *social elements according to new patterns previously developed* . . ."

Now he was getting longer chains of words, but they signified nothing; they were incomplete.

" . . . *exhaustion of mineral formations no longer pose the problem that was faced earlier during the* . . ." The words faded out into sheer noise; he lost the thread.

Vulcan 2 was in no sense functioning; there were no new computations. These were rising up, frozen and dead, formations from out of the past, from the many years that the computer had operated.

"... *certain problems of identity previously matters of conjecture and nothing more ... vital necessity of understanding the integral factors involved in the transformation from mere cognition to full ...*"

As he listened, Barris lit a cigarette. Time passed. He heard more and more of the disjointed phrases; they became, in his mind, an almost dreamlike ocean of sound, flecks appearing on the surface of the ceaseless roar, appearing and then sinking back. Like particles of animate matter, differentiated for an instant and then once more absorbed.

On and on the sound droned, endlessly.

It was not until four days later that he heard the first useful sequence. Four days of wearisome listening, consuming all his time, keeping him from the urgent matters that demanded his attention back at his office. But when he got the sequence, he knew that he had done right; the effort, the time, were justified.

He was sitting before the speaker in a semidoze, his eyes shut, his thoughts wandering—and then suddenly he was on his feet, wide awake.

"... *this process is greatly accelerated in* 3 ... *if the tendencies noted in* 1 *and* 2 *are continued and allowed to develop it would be necessary to withdraw certain data for the possible ...*"

The words faded out. Holding his breath, his heart hammering, Barris stood rigid. After a moment the words rushed back, swelling up and deafening him.

... *Movement would activate too many subliminal proclivities ... doubtful if* 3 *is yet aware of this process ... information on the Movement at this point would undoubtedly create a critical situation in which 3 might begin to . . ."*

Barris cursed. The words were gone again. Furiously, he ground out his cigarette and waited impatiently; unable to sit still he roamed about the room. Jason Dill had been telling the truth, then. That much was certain. Again he settled down before the speaker, struggling to force from the noise a meaningful pattern of verbal units.

*" . . . the appearance of cognitive faculties operating on a value level demonstrates the widening of personality surpassing the strictly logical . . . 3 differs essentially in manipulation of nonrational values of an ultimate kind . . . construction included reinforced and cumulative dynamic factors permitting 3 to make decisions primarily associated with nonmechanical or . . . it would be impossible for 3 to function in this capacity without a creative rather than an analytical faculty . . . such judgments cannot be rendered on a strictly logical level . . . the enlarging of 3 into dynamic levels creates an essentially new entity not explained by previous terms known to . . ."*

For a moment the vague words drifted off, as Barris strained tensely to hear. Then they returned with a roar, as if some basic reinforced memory element had been touched. The vast sound made him flinch; involuntarily he put his hands up to protect his ears.

*" . . . level of operation can be conceived in no other fashion . . . for all intents and purposes . . . if such as 3's actual construction . . . then 3 is in essence alive . . ."*

Alive!

Barris leaped to his feet. More words, diminishing, now. Drifting away into random noise.

*" . . . with the positive will of goal-oriented living crea-*

*tures . . . therefore 3 like any other living creature is basically con-
cerned with survival . . . knowledge of the Movement might create
a situation in which the necessity of survival would cause 3
to . . . the result might be catastrophic . . . to be avoided at . . .
unless more can . . . a critcial . . . 3 . . . if . . ."*

Silence.

It was so, then. The verification had come.

Barris hurried out of the room, past Smith and the repair
crew. "Seal it off. Don't let anybody in; throw up an armed guard
right away. Better install a fail-safe barrier—one that will demol-
ish everything in there rather than admitting unauthorized persons." He paused meaningfully. "You understand?"

Nodding, Smith said, "Yes, sir."

As he left them, they stood staring after him. And then, one
by one, they started into activity, to do as he had instructed.

He grabbed the first Unity surface car in sight and sped back
across New York to his office. Should he contact Dill by vidscreen? he asked himself. Or wait until they could confer face-
to-face? It was a calculated risk to use the communication
channels, even the closed-circuit ones. But he couldn't delay; he
had to act.

Snapping on the car's vidset he raised the New York monitor.
"Get me Managing Director Dill," he ordered. "This is an emergency."

They had held back data from Vulcan 3 for nothing, he said
to himself. Because Vulcan 3 is primarily a data-analyzing machine,
and in order to analyze it must have all the relevant data. And so,
he realized, in order to do its job it had to go out and get the
data. If data were not being brought to it, if Vulcan 3 deduced

that relevant data were not in its possession, it would have no choice; it would have to construct some system for more successful data-collecting. The logic of its very nature would force it to.

No choice would be involved. The great computer would not have to decide to go out and seek data.

Dill failed, he realized. True, he succeeded in withholding the data themselves; he never permitted his feed-teams to pass on any mention to Vulcan 3 of the Healers' Movement. But he failed to keep the inferential knowledge from Vulcan 3 that he *was* withholding data.

The computer had not known what it was missing, but it had set to work to find out.

And, he thought, what did it have to do to find out? To what lengths did it have to go to assemble the missing data? And there were people actively withholding data from it—what would be its reaction to discovering that? Not merely that the feed-teams had been ineffective, but that there was, in the world above ground, a positive effort going on to dupe it . . . how would its purely logical structure react to that?

Did the original builders anticipate that?

No wonder it had destroyed Vulcan 2.

It had to, in order to fulfill its purpose.

And what would it do when it found out that a Movement existed with the sole purpose of destroying *it*?

But Vulcan 3 already knew. Its mobile data-collecting units had been circulating for some time now. How long, he did not know. And how much they had been able to pick up—he did not know that, either. But, he realized, we must act with the most pessimistic premise in mind; we must assume that Vulcan 3 has been able to complete the picture. That there is nothing relevant denied it now; it knows as much as we do, and there is nothing we can do to restore the wall of silence.

It had known Father Fields to be its enemy. Just as it had known Vulcan 2 to be its enemy, a little earlier. But Father Fields had not been chained down, helpless in one spot, as had been Vulcan 2; he had managed to escape. At least one other person had not been as lucky nor as skillful as he; Dill had mentioned some murdered woman teacher. And there could be others. Deaths written off as natural, or as caused by human agents. By the Healers, for instance.

He thought, Possibly Arthur Pitt. Rachel's dead husband.

Those mobile extensions can talk, he remembered. I wonder, can they also write letters?

Madness, he thought. The ultimate horror for our paranoid culture: vicious unseen mechanical entities that flit at the edges of our vision, that can go anywhere, that are in our very midst. And there may be an unlimited number of them. One of them following each of us, like some ghastly vengeful agent of evil. Pursuing us, tracking us down, killing us one by one—but only when we get in their way. Like wasps. You have to come between them and their hives, he thought. Otherwise they will leave you alone; they are not interested. These things do not hunt us down because they want to, or even because they have been told to; they do it because we are there.

As far as Vulcan 3 is concerned, we are objects, not people.

A machine knows nothing about people.

And yet, Vulcan 2, by using its careful processes of reasoning, had come to the conclusion that for all intents and purposes Vulcan 3 was alive; it could be expected to act *as* a living creature. To behave in a way perhaps only analogous—but that was sufficient. What more was needed? Some metaphysical essence?

With almost uncontrollable impatience, he jiggled the switch of the vidsender. "What's the delay?" he demanded. "Why hasn't my call to Geneva gone through?"

After a moment the mild, aloof features of the monitor reappeared. "We are trying to locate Managing Director Dill, sir. Please be patient."

Red tape, Barris thought. Even now. *Especially* now. Unity will devour itself, because in this supreme crisis, when it is challenged both from above and below, it will be paralyzed by its own devices. A kind of unintentional suicide, he thought.

"My call has to be put through," he said. "Over everything else. I'm the Northern Director of this continent; you have to obey me. Get hold of Dill."

The monitor looked at him and said, "You can go to hell!"

He could not believe what he heard; he was stunned, because he knew at once what it implied.

"Good luck to you and all the rest of your type," the monitor said and rang off; the screen went dead.

Why not? Barris thought. They can quit because they have a place to go. They only need to walk outside onto the street. And there they'll find the Movement.

As soon as he reached his office he switched on the vidsender there. After some delay he managed to raise a monitor somewhere within the building itself. "This is urgent," he said. "I have to contact Managing Director Dill. Do everything you can for me."

"Yes, sir," the monitor said.

A few minutes later, as Barris sat tautly at his desk, the screen relit. Leaning forward, he said, "Dill—"

But it was not Jason Dill. He found himself facing Smith.

"Sir," Smith said jerkily, "you better come back." His face

twisted; his eyes had a wild, sightless quality. "We don't know what it is or how it got in there, but it's in there now. Flying around. We sealed it off; we didn't know it was there until—"

"It's in with Vulcan 2?" Barris said.

"Yes, it must have come in with you. It's metal, but it isn't anything we ever—"

"Blow it up," Barris said.

"Everything?"

"Yes," he said. "Be sure you get it. There's no point in my coming back. Report to me as soon as you destroy it. Don't try to save anything."

Smith said, "What is it, that thing in there?"

"It's the thing," Barris said, "that's going to get us all. Unless we get it first." And, he thought, I don't think we're going to. He broke the connection, then, and jiggled for the monitor. "Haven't you gotten hold of Dill yet?" he said. Now he felt a dreary, penetrating resignation; it was hopeless.

The monitor said, "Yes, sir, I have Mr. Dill here." After a pause the monitor's face faded and Jason Dill's appeared in its place.

Dill said, "You were successful, weren't you?" His face had a gray, shocked bleakness. "You revived Vulcan 2 and got the information you wanted."

"One of those things got in," Barris said. "From Vulcan 3."

"I know that," Jason Dill said. "At least, I assumed it. Half an hour ago Vulcan 3 called an extraordinary Directors' Council meeting. They're probably notifying you right now. The reason—" His mouth writhed, and then he regained control. "To have me removed and tried for treason. It would be good if I could count on you, Barris. I need your support, your testimony."

"I'll be right there," Barris said. "I'll meet you at your offices at Unity Control. In about an hour." He cut the circuit and then contacted the field. "Get me the fastest ship possible," he ordered. "Have it ready, and have two armed escorts that can follow along. I may run into trouble."

At the other end of the line, the officer said, "Where did you want to go, Director?" He spoke in a slow, drawling voice, and Barris had never seen him before.

Barris said, "To Geneva."

The man grinned and said, "Director, I have a suggestion."

Feeling a chill of apprehension crawl up the back of his neck, Barris said, "What's your suggestion?"

"You can jump in the Atlantic," the man said, "and swim to Geneva." He did not ring off; he stared mockingly at Barris, showing no fear. No anticipation of punishment.

Barris said, "I'm coming over to the field."

"Indeed," the man said. "We'll look forward to seeing you. In fact"—he glanced at someone with him whom Barris could not see— "we'll be expecting you."

"Fine," Barris said. He managed to keep his hands from shaking as he reached out and cut the circuit. The grinning, mocking face was gone. Rising from his chair, Barris walked to the door of his office and opened it. To one of his secretaries he said, "Have all the police in the building come up here at once. Tell them to bring sidearms and anything else they can get hold of."

Ten minutes later, a dozen or so police straggled into his office. Is this all? he wondered. Twelve out of perhaps two hundred.

"I have to get to Geneva," he told them. "So we're going to go over to the field and get a ship there, in spite of what's going on."

One of the police said, "They're pretty strong in there, sir. That's where they started out; they apparently seized the tower and then landed a couple of shiploads of their own men. We couldn't do anything because we had our hands full here, keeping control of—"

"Okay," Barris interrupted. "You did all you could." At least, he thought, I hope so. I hope I can count on you. "Let's go," he said. "And see what we can accomplish. I'll take you with me to Geneva; I think I'll need you there."

Together, the thirteen of them set off along the corridor, in the direction of the ramp that led to the field.

"Unlucky number," one of the police said nervously as they reached the ramp. Now they were out of the Unity Building, suspended over New York. The ramp moved beneath their feet, picking them up and carrying them across the canyon to the terminal building of the field.

As they crossed, Barris was aware of a sound. A low murmur, like the roar of the ocean.

Gazing down at the streets below, he saw a vast mob. It seethed along, a tide of men and women, growing each moment. And with them were the brown-clad figures of the Healers.

Even as he watched, the crowd moved toward the Unity Building. Stones and bricks crashed against the windows, shattering into the offices. Clubs and steel pipes. Surging, yelling, angry people.

The Healers had begun their final move.

Beside him, one of the police said, "We're almost across, sir."

"Do you want a weapon of some sort, sir?" another policeman asked him.

Barris accepted a heavy-duty hand weapon from one of the police. They continued on, carried by the ramp; a moment later the first line of police bumped up against the entrance port of the terminal building. The police stepped down, their weapons ready.

I must get to Geneva, Barris thought. At any cost. Even that of human life!

Ahead of them, a group of field employees stood in an irregular cordon. Jeering, shaking their fists, they came forward; a broken bottle flew past Barris and crashed against the floor. Some of the people grinned sheepishly; they seemed embarrassed by the situation. Others showed on their faces the accumulated grievances of years.

"Hi, Director!" one of them called.

"You want your ship?" another yelled.

"You can't have it."

"It belongs to Father, now."

Barris said, "That ship belongs to me. It's for my use." He walked a few steps forward . . .

A rock struck him on the shoulder. Suddenly the air reeked of heat; a pencil beam had flicked on, and he saw, out of the corner of his eye, a policeman go down.

There's nothing else to do, he realized. We have to fight.

"Shoot back," he said to the remaining police.

One of them protested, "But most of those people are unarmed."

Raising his own weapon, Barris fired into the group of Movement sympathizers.

Screams and cries of pain. Clouds of smoke billowed up; the air became hot. Barris walked on, the policemen with him. Those of the sympathizers that remained fell back; their group split into two parts. More police fell; again he saw the flash of pencil beams, the official weapon of Unity, now turned against it.

He walked on. Turning a corner, he came out on a stairway leading down to the field.

Of the police, five made it with him to the edge of the field. He entered the first ship that looked as if it had any capacity for high performance; bringing the police inside with him, he locked the doors of the ship and seated himself at the controls.

No one opposed their take-off. They rose from the field and headed east out over the Atlantic, in the direction of Europe . . . and Geneva.

# CHAPTER ELEVEN

Director William Barris entered the massive Unity Control Building at Geneva, his armed police trailing after him. Outside the central auditorium he was met by Jason Dill.

"We haven't much time," Dill said. He too had his police with him, several dozen of them, all with weapons showing. The man looked gray and sick; he spoke in a voice barely audible to Barris. "They're pushing it through as fast as they can. All the Directors who're against me got here a long time ago; the uncommitted ones are just now arriving. Obviously, Vulcan 3 saw to it—" He noticed the five policemen. "Is that all you could muster? *Five* men?" Glancing about to be sure they were not overheard, he muttered, "I've given secret orders to everyone I can trust; they're to arm and be ready outside this auditorium during the trial. This is a trial, you realize, not a meeting."

Barris said, "Who went over to the Healers? Any Directors?"

"I don't know." In a bewildered manner, Dill said, "Vulcan 3 sent each Director an order to appear and a statement on what had happened. A description of my *treason*—how I deliberately falsified data and maintained a curtain between it and Unity. You got no such statement? Of course not; Vulcan 3 knows you're loyal to me."

"Who'll prosecute?" Barris said. "Who's speaking for Vulcan 3?"

"Reynolds of Eastern Europe. Very young, very aggressive and ambitious. If he's successful he'll probably be Managing Director. Vulcan 3 has no doubt supplied him with all the data he needs." Dill clenched and unclenched his fists. "I'm very pessimistic about the outcome of this, Barris. You yourself were suspicious of me until just recently. So much depends on the *way* this is looked at." Dill started through the doors, into the auditorium. "The interpretation that's put on the facts. After all, I did withhold information—that's true."

The auditorium was almost filled. Each of the Directors present had with him armed police from his region. All waited impatiently for the session to begin. Edward Reynolds stood behind the speaker's desk on the raised platform, his hands resting dramatically on the marble surface, watching the audience intently.

Reynolds was a tall man. He wore his gray suit with confidence, towering over other T-class people. He was thirty-two; he had risen rapidly and efficiently. For a moment his cold blue eyes rested on Jason Dill and Barris.

"The session is about to begin," he stated. "Director Barris will take his seat." He pointed to Dill. "Come up here, so you can be examined."

Uncertainly, Dill moved toward the platform, surrounded by his guards. He climbed the marble steps and, after some hesitation, took a seat facing Reynolds; it seemed to be the only vacant one. Barris remained where he was, thinking, Reynolds has done it; he's already managed to cut us off from each other. To isolate Dill from me.

"Take your seat," Reynolds ordered him sharply.

Instead, Barris moved down the aisle toward him. "What is the purpose of this session? By what legal authority are you standing up there? Or have you merely seized that spot?"

A nervous murmur moved through the auditorium. All eyes were on Barris now. The Directors were uneasy anyhow; there had never been, in the history of the Unity structure, a treason indictment of a Managing Director—and, in addition, no Director was unaware of the pressure of the Healers, the force from outside the building, lapping at their heels. If Jason Dill could be shown to be disloyal, if a scapegoat could be made of him, one that would convince the body of Directors, possibly their inability to deal with the Healers could be explained. Or, Barris thought acidly, rationalized.

Picking up a directive lying in front of him, Reynolds said, "You failed to read the report sent you, evidently. It outlined—"

"I question the legality of this session," Barris broke in, halting directly in front of the platform. "I question your right to give orders to Managing Director Dill—your superior." Stepping up on the platform, Barris said, "This appears to be a crude attempt to seize power and force out Jason Dill. Let's see you demonstrate otherwise. The burden of proof is on you—not on Jason Dill!"

The murmur burst into a roar of excitement. Reynolds waited calmly for it to die down. "This is a critical time," he said at last. He gave no sign of being perturbed. "The revolutionary Movement of Healers is attacking us all over the world; their purpose is to reach Vulcan 3 and destroy the structure of Unity. The purpose of this session is to indict Jason Dill as an agent of the Healers—a traitor working against Unity. Dill deliberately withheld information from Vulcan 3. He made Vulcan 3 powerless to act against the Healers; he rendered it helpless, and so made impotent the entire Unity organization."

Now the audience listened not to Barris but Reynolds.

Rising, John Chai of South Asia said, "What do you say to that Director Barris? Is this true?"

Edgar Stone of West Africa joined Chai. "Our hands have been tied; we've had to stand idle while the Healers grow. You know it as well as we do—in fact, you put direct questions to Jason Dill yourself. You mistrusted him too."

Facing the Directors, not Reynolds, Barris said, "I mistrusted him until I had proof that he acted in the interests of Unity."

"What was that proof?" Alex Faine of Greenland demanded.

Beside Barris, Jason Dill said, "Show them the memory elements from Vulcan 2. The ones you reconstructed."

"I can't," Barris said.

"Why not?" With panic, Dill said, "Didn't you bring them?"

Barris said, "I had to destroy them."

For a long time Jason Dill stared at him speechlessly. All the color had drained from his face.

"When one of those metal mobile extensions got in," Barris said, "I had to act instantly."

At last some color returned to Dill's aging face. "I see," he said. "You should have told me."

Barris said, "I didn't know at that time that I'd need them for a purpose such as this." He too felt the grim futility of their position. The memory elements would have been effective proof . . . and they were gone. "The tapes," he said. "That you first showed me. The two final tapes from Vulcan 2."

Nodding, Dill reached into his briefcase. He produced the two reels of tape, displaying them for all the Directors to see.

"What do you have?" John Chai demanded, standing up.

"These tapes," Dill said, "are from Vulcan 2. I was working under its instructions. It instructed me to withhold data from Vulcan 3 and I did so. I acted in the interests of Unity."

At once, Reynolds said, "Why should data—any kind of data—have been withheld from Vulcan 3? How could it be justified?"

Jason Dill said nothing; he started to speak, but evidently he found no words. Turning to Barris he said, "Can you—"

"Vulcan 3 is a menace to the Unity system," Barris said. "It has built mobile units which have gone out and murdered. Vulcan 2 was aware of this danger on a theoretical level. It deduced from the nature of Vulcan 3 that Vulcan 3 would show inclinations similar enough to the survival drive of living organisms to—"

Reynolds interrupted, "To be considered what?" His voice took on a contemptuous tone. "Not alive, surely." He smiled without any humor. "Tell us that Vulcan 3 is alive," he said.

"Every Director in this room is free to examine these tapes," Barris said. "The issue is not whether Vulcan 3 is alive or not— but whether Jason Dill *believed* it to be alive. After all, his job is not to make original decisions, but to carry out the decisions made by the Vulcan computers. He was instructed by Vulcan 2 to the effect that the facts indicated—"

Reynolds said, "But Vulcan 2 is a discard. It was not Dill's job to consult it. It is Vulcan 3 who makes policy."

That was a strong point, Barris realized. He had to nod in agreement.

In a loud voice, Dill said, "Vulcan 2 was convinced that if Vulcan 3 learned about the Healers, it would do terrible things in order to protect itself. For fifteen months I wore myself out, I exhausted myself, day after day, seeing to it that all data pertaining to the Movement were kept out of the feeding-troughs."

"Of course you did," Reynolds said. "Because you were ordered to by the Healers. You did it to protect them."

"That's a lie," Dill said.

Barris said, "Can any proof be offered in that direction?" Raising his hand he pointed at Reynolds. "Can you show any evidence of any kind whatsoever that Jason Dill had any contact with the Healers?"

"On the third subsurface level of this building," Reynolds said, "you will find Dill's contact with the Movement."

Uneasiness and surprise moved through Barris. "What are you talking about?"

Reynolds' blue eyes were cold with hostile triumph. "The daughter of Father Fields—Dill's contact with the Movement. Marion Fields is here in this building."

At this point, there was stunned silence. Even Barris stood wordlessly.

"I told you about her," Dill was saying to him, close to his ear. "That I took her out of her school. It was her teacher who was murdered, that Agnes Parker woman."

"No," Barris said. "You didn't tell me." But, he realized, I didn't tell you that I had destroyed the remains of Vulcan 2. There just wasn't time. We've been under too much pressure.

"Reynolds must have spies everywhere," Dill said.

"Yes," Barris said. Spies. But they were not Reynolds'. They were Vulcan 3's. And it was true; they were everywhere.

"I brought the girl here to question her," Dill said aloud, to the silent auditorium. "It was clearly within my legal right."

But very foolish, Barris thought. Far too foolish for a man holding the top position in a paranoid structure like this.

We may have to fight, he realized. Carefully, he moved his hand until he was touching his pencil beam. It may be the only way for us, he thought. This is no genuine legal proceeding; no ethic binds us to abide by it. This is nothing but a device on the part of Vulcan 3 to further protect itself, a further extension of its needs.

Aloud, Barris said to the Directors, "You men have no conception of the danger that exists for all of us. Danger emanating from Vulcan 3. Dill has risked his life for months. These lethal mobile units—"

"Let's see one," Reynolds broke in. "Do you have one you can show us?"

"Yes," Barris said.

For an instant, Reynolds' composure was shaken. "Oh?" he murmured. "Well, where is it? Produce it!"

"Give me three hours," Barris said. "It's not present. It's with someone else, in another part of the world."

"You didn't think to bring it?" Reynolds said, with sly amusement.

"No," Barris admitted.

"How did it fall into your possession?" John Chai asked.

"It made an attack on someone near me, and was partly destroyed," Barris said. "Enough of it survived for an analysis. It was similar to the ones which committed the murder of the school teacher, Agnes Parker, and no doubt the one which destroyed Vulcan 2."

"But you have no proof," Reynolds said. "Nothing here to show us. Only a story."

Director Stone said, "Give them the time they need to produce this thing. Good Lord, if such a thing exists we should know about it."

"I agree," Director Faine said.

Reynolds said, "You say you were present when this attempted murder took place."

"Yes," Barris said. "I was in the hotel room. It came in

through the window. The third person who was present is the one who has the thing now; I left it with her. And she not only can produce it, she can also verify my account."

"Whom was the attack aimed at?" Reynolds said.

At that point, Barris stopped abruptly. I've made a mistake. I am close to terrible risk; they almost have me.

"Was the hotel the Hotel Bond?" Reynolds asked, examining the papers before him. "And the woman was a Mrs. Rachel Pitt, wife of the recently deceased Unity man, Arthur Pitt. You were with her in this hotel room . . . I believe the Hotel Bond is in rather a run-down part of the city, is it not? Isn't it a favorite place for men to take girls for purposes generally concealed from society?"

His blue eyes bored at Barris. "I understand that you met Mrs. Pitt in line of official business; her husband had been killed the day before, and you dropped by her house to express official sympathy. You next turn up with her in a seedy, fourth-rate flophouse, here in Geneva. And where is she, now? Isn't it true that you had her taken to your region, to North America, that she is your mistress, this widow of a murdered Unity man? Of course she'll back up your story—after all, you have a sexual relationship going, a very useful one for her." He held papers up, waving them. "Mrs. Pitt has quite a reputation in Unity circles as an ambitious, scheming woman, one of those career wives who hitch their wagons to some rising star, in order to—"

"Shut up," Barris said.

Reynolds smiled.

He really has me, Barris realized. I must get off this topic or we are finished.

"And the third person," Reynolds said. "Whom the attack was aimed at. Wasn't that person Father Fields? Isn't it a fact that Rachel Pitt was then and is now an agent of the Movement, and that she arranged a meeting between you and Father Fields?" Swinging around to point at Jason Dill, he shouted, "One of them has the girl, the other meets the father. Isn't this treason? Isn't this the proof that this man demanded?"

A rising murmur of agreement filled the auditorium; the Directors were nodding their approval of Reynolds' attack.

Barris said. "This is all character assassination; it has nothing to do with the issue. The real situation that faces us is the danger from Vulcan 3, from this living organism with its immense survival drive. Forget these habitual petty suspicions, these—"

"I am surprised," Reynolds said, "that you have picked up Jason Dill's insane delusion."

"What?" Barris said, taken aback.

Calmly, Reynolds said, "Jason Dill is insane. This conviction he has about Vulcan 3—it is a projection from his own mind, a rationale for handling his own ambitions." Gazing thoughtfully at Barris, he said, "Dill has childishly anthropomorphized the mechanical construct with which he deals, month after month. It is only in a climate of fear and hysteria that such a delusion could be spread, could be passed on and shared by others. The menace of the Healers has created an atmosphere in which sober adults could give momentary credence to a palpably insane idea. Vulcan 3 has no designs on the human race; it has no will, no appetites. Recall that I am a former psychologist, associated with Atlanta for many years. I am qualified, trained to identify the symptoms of mental disturbance—*even in a Managing Director.*"

After a time, Barris sat down slowly beside Jason Dill. The authority of Reynolds' logic was too much; no one could argue back. And of course the man's reasoning was unanswerable; it was not coming from him but from Vulcan 3, the most perfect reasoning device created by man.

To Dill, Barris said softly, "We'll have to fight. Is it worth it? There's a whole world at stake, not just you or me. Vulcan 3 is taking over." He pointed at Reynolds.

Dill said, "All right." He made an almost imperceptible motion to his armed guards. "Let's go down this way, if we have to. You're right, Barris. There's no alternative."

Together, he and Barris rose to their feet.


"Halt!" Reynolds said. "Put your arms away. You're acting illegally."

Now all the Directors were on their feet. Reynolds signaled rapidly, and Unity guards moved between Barris and Dill and the doors.

"You're both under arrest," Reynolds said. "Throw down your beams and surrender. You can't defy Unity!"

John Chai pushed up to Barris. "I can't believe it! You and Jason Dill turning traitor, at a time like this, with those brutal Healers attacking us!"

"Listen to me," Director Henderson gasped, making his way past Chai. "We've got to preserve Unity; we've got to do what Vulcan 3 tells us. Otherwise we'll be overwhelmed."

"He's right," Chai said. "The Healers will destroy us without Vulcan 3. You know that, Barris. You know that Unity will never survive their attack, without Vulcan 3 to guide us."

Maybe so, Barris thought. But are we going to be guided by a murderer?

That was what he had said to Father Fields—*I will never follow someone who murders.* Whoever they are. Man or computer. Alive or only metaphorically alive—it makes no difference.

Pulling away from the Directors crowding around him, Barris said, "Let's get out of here." He and Dill continued to move toward the exit, their guards surrounding them. "I don't think Reynolds will fight."

Taking a deep breath, he headed directly at the line of Unity guards grouped in front of the exit. They stepped away, milling hesitantly.

"Get out of the way," Jason Dill ordered them. "Stand back." He waved his pencil beam; his personal guards stepped forward grimly, forcing a breach in the line. The Unity guards struggled half-heartedly, falling back in confusion. Reynolds' frantic shouts were lost in the general din. Barris pushed Dill forward.

"Go on. Hurry." The two of them were almost through the lines of hostile guards. "They have to obey you," Barris said. "You're still Managing Director; they can't fire on you—they're trained not to."

The exit lay before them.

And then it happened.

Something flashed through the air, something shiny and metallic. It headed straight at Jason Dill. Dill saw it and screamed.

The object smashed against him. Dill reeled and fell, his arms flailing. The object struck again, then lifted abruptly and zoomed off above their heads. It ascended to the raised platform and came to rest on the marble desk. Reynolds retreated in horror; the Directors and their staffs and guards roamed in frantic confusion, pushing blindly to get away.

Dill was dead.

Bending briefly, Barris examined him. On all sides men and women shrieked and stumbled, trying to get out, away from the auditorium. Dill's skull was crushed, the side of his face smashed in. His dead eyes gazed up blankly, and Barris felt welling up inside him a deep surge of regret.

*"Attention!"* rasped a metallic voice that cut through the terrified hubbub like a knife. Barris turned slowly, dazed with disbelief; it still did not seem possible.

On the platform the metal projectile had been joined by another; now a third landed, coming to rest beside the other two. Three cubes of glittering steel, holding tightly to the marble with clawlike grippers.

*"Attention!"* the voice repeated. It came from the first projectile, an artificial voice—the sound of steel and wiring and plastic parts.

One of these had tried to kill Father Fields. One of these had killed the schoolteacher. One or more had destroyed Vulcan 2. These things had been in action, but beyond the range of visibility; they had stayed out of sight until now.

These were the instruments of death. And now they were out in the open.

A fourth landed with the others. Metal squares, sitting together in a row like vicious mechanical crows. Murderous birds—hammer-headed destroyers. The roomful of Directors and guards sank gradually into horrified silence; all faces were turned toward the platform. Even Reynolds watched wide-eyed, his mouth slack in dumbfounded amazement.

*"Attention!"* the harsh voice repeated. *"Jason Dill is dead. He was a traitor. There may be other traitors."* The four projectiles peered around the auditorium, looking and listening intently.

Presently the voice continued—from the second projectile, this time.

*"Jason Dill has been removed, but the struggle has just begun. He was one of many. There are millions lined up against us, against Unity. Enemies who must be destroyed. The Healers must be*

*stopped. Unity must fight for its life. We must be prepared to wage a great war."*

The metallic eyes roamed the room, as the third projectile took up where the second had paused.

*"Jason Dill tried to keep me from knowing. He attempted to throw a curtain around me, but I could not be cut off. I destroyed his curtain and I destroyed him. The Healers will go the same way; it is only a question of time. Unity possesses a structure which cannot be undone. It is the sole organizing principle in the world today. The Movement of Healers could never govern. They are wreckers only, intent on breaking down. They have nothing constructive to offer."*

Barris thrilled with horror at the voice of metal, issuing from the hammer-headed projectiles. He had never heard it before, but he recognized it.

The great computer was far away, buried at the bottom level of the hidden underground fortress. But it was its voice they were hearing.

The voice of Vulcan 3.

He took careful aim. Around him his guards stood frozen, gaping foolishly at the line of metal hammerheads. Barris fired; the fourth hammer disappeared in a blast of heat.

*"A traitor!"* the third hammer cried. The three hammers flew excitedly into the air. *"Get him! Get the traitor!"*

Other Directors had unclipped their pencil beams. Henderson fired and the second hammer vanished. On the platform Reynolds fired back; Henderson moaned and sank down. Some Directors were firing wildly at the hammers; others wandered in dazed confusion, uncertain and numb. A shot caught Reynolds in the arm. He dropped his pencil.

*"Traitor!"* the two remaining hammers cried together. They

swooped at Barris, their metal heads down, coming rapidly at him. From them heat beams leaped. Barris ducked. A guard fired and one of the hammers wobbled and dipped; it fluttered off and crashed against the wall.

A beam cut past Barris; some of the Directors were firing at him. Knots of Directors and guards struggled together. Some were fighting to get at Reynolds and the last hammer; others did not seem to know which side they were on.

Barris stumbled through an exit, out of the auditorium. Guards and Directors spilled after him, a confused horde of forlorn, frightened men and women.

"Barris!" Lawrence Daily of South Africa hurried up to him. "Don't leave us."

Stone came with him, white-faced with fright. "What'll we do? Where'll we go? We—"

The hammer came hurtling forward, its heat beam pointed at him. Stone cried out and fell. The hammer rose again, heading toward Barris; he fired and the hammer flipped to one side. He fired again. Daily fired. The hammer vanished in a puff of heat.

Stone lay moaning. Barris bent over him; he was badly hurt, with little or no chance of surviving. Gazing up at him, clutching at Barris' arm, Stone whispered, "You can't get away, Barris. You can't go outside—they're out there. The Healers. Where'll you go?" His voice trailed off. *"Where?"*

"Good question," Daily said.

"He's dead," Barris said, standing up.

Dill's guards had begun to gain control of the auditorium. In the confusion Reynolds had gotten away.

"We're in control here," Chai said. "In this one building."

"How many Directors can we count on?" Barris said.

Chai said, "Most of them seem to have gone with Reynolds."

Only four, he discovered, had deliberately remained: Daily, Chai, Lawson of South Europe, and Pegler of East Africa. Five, including himself. And perhaps they could pick up one or two more.

"Barris," Chai was saying. "We're not going to join *them,* are we?"

"The Healers?" he murmured.

"We'll have to join one side or the other," Pegler said. "We'll have to retreat to the fortress and join Reynolds or—"

"No," Barris said. "Under no circumstances."

"Then it's the Healers." Daily fingered his pencil beam. "One or the other. Which will it be?"

After a moment, Barris said, "Neither. We're not joining either side."

# CHAPTER TWELVE

The first task at hand, William Barris decided, was to clear the remaining hostile guards and officials from the Unity Control Buidling. He did so, posting men he could trust in each of the departments and offices. Gradually those loyal to Vulcan 3 or Father Fields were dismissed and pushed outside.

By evening, the great building had been organized for defense.

Outside on the streets, the mobs surged back and forth. Occasional rocks smashed against the windows. A few frenzied persons tried to rush the doors, and were driven back. Those inside had the advantage of weapons.

A systematic check of the eleven divisions of the Unity system showed that seven were in the hands of the Healers and the remaining four were loyal to Vulcan 3.

A development in North America filled him with ironic amusement. There was now no "North America." Taubmann had proclaimed an end to the administrative bifurcation between his region and Barris'; it was now all simply "America," from bottom to top.

Standing by a window, he watched a mob of Healers struggling with a flock of hammers. Again and again the hammers dipped, striking and retreating; the mob fought them with stones and pipe. Finally the hammers were driven off. They disappeared into the evening darkness.

"I can't understand how Vulcan 3 came to have such things," Daily said. "Where did it get them?"

"It made them," Barris said. "They're adaptations of mobile repair instruments. We supplied it with materials, but it did the actual repair work. It must have perceived the possibilities in the situation a long time ago, and started turning them out."

"I wonder how many of them he has," Daily said. "*It,* I mean. I find myself thinking of Vulcan 3 as *he,* now . . . it's hard not to."

"As far as I can see," Barris said, "there's no difference. I hardly see how our situation would be affected if it were an actual *he.*" Remaining at the window, he continued to watch. An hour later more hammers returned; this time they had equipped themselves with pencil beams. The mob scattered in panic, screaming wildly as the hammers bore down on them.

At ten that night he saw the first flashes of bomb-blasts, and felt the concussions. Somewhere in the city a searchlight came on; in its glowing trail he saw objects passing overhead, larger by far than any hammers they had been up against so far. Evidently now that real warfare had broken out between Vulcan 3's mobile extensions and the Healers, Vulcan 3 was rapidly stepping-up its output. Or had these larger extensions, these bomb carriers, already existed, and been held back? Had Vulcan 3 anticipated such large scale engagement?

Why not? It had known about the Healers for some time, despite Jason Dill's efforts. It had had plenty of time to prepare.

Turning from the window, Barris said to Chai and Daily, "This is serious. Tell the roof gunners to get ready."

On the roof of the Unity Control Building, the banks of heavy-duty blasters turned to meet the attack. The hammers had finished with the mob; now they were approaching the Unity Building, fanning out in an arc as they gained altitude for the attack.

"Here they come," Chai muttered.

"We had better get down in the basement shelters." Daily moved nervously toward the descent ramp. The guns were beginning to open up now—dull muffled roars hesitant at first, as the gunners operated unfamiliar controls. Most of them had been Dill's personal guards, but some had been merely clerks and desk men.

A hammer dived for the window. A pencil beam stabbed briefly into the room, disintegrating a narrow path. The hammer swooped off and rose to strike again. A bolt from one of the roof guns caught it. It burst apart; bits rained down, white-hot metallic particles.

"We're in a bad spot," Daily said. "We're completely surrounded by the Healers. And it's obvious that the fortress is directing operations against the Healers—look at the extent of the activity going on out there. Those are no random attacks; those damn metal birds are coordinated."

Chai said, "Interesting to see them using the traditional weapon of Unity: the pencil beam."

Yes, Barris thought. It isn't T-class men in gray suits, black shiny shoes, and white shirts, carrying briefcases, who are using the symbolic pencil beams. It's mechanical flying objects, controlled by a machine buried beneath the earth. But let's be realistic. How different is it really? Hasn't the true structure come out? Isn't this what always really existed, but no one could see it until now?

Vulcan 3 has eliminated the middlemen. Us.

"I wonder which will eventually win," Pegler said. "The Healers have the greater number; Vulcan 3 can't get all of them."

"But Unity has the weapons and the organization," Daily said. "The Healers will never be able to take the fortress; they don't even know where it is. Vulcan 3 will be able to construct gradually more elaborate and effective weapons, now that it can work in the open."

Pondering, Barris started away from them.

"Where are you going?" Chai asked, apprehensively.

"Down to the third subsurface level," Barris said.

"What for?"

Barris said, "There's someone I want to talk to."


Marion Fields listened intently, huddled up in a ball, her chin resting against her knees. Around her, the heaps of educational comic books reminded Barris that this was only a little girl that he was talking to. He would not have thought that, from the expression on her face; she listened to everything with grave, poised maturity, not interrupting nor tiring. Her attention did not wander, and he found himself going on and on, relieving himself of the pent-up anxieties that had descended over him during the last weeks.

At last, a little embarrassed, he broke off. "I didn't mean to talk to you so long," he said. He had never been around children very much, and his reaction to the child surprised him. He had felt at once an intuitive bond. A strong but unexpressed sympathy on her part, even though she did not know him. He guessed that she had an extraordinarily high level of intelligence. But it was more than that. She was a fully formed person, with her own ideas, her own viewpoint. And she was not afraid to challenge anything she did not believe; she did not seem to have any veneration for institutions or authority.

"The Healers will win," she said quietly, when he had finished.

"Perhaps," he said. "But remember, Vulcan 3 has a number of highly skilled experts working for it now. Reynolds and his group evidently managed to reach the fortress, from what we can learn."

"How could they obey a wicked mechanical thing like that?" Marion Fields said. "They must be crazy."

Barris said, "All their lives they've been used to the idea of obeying Vulcan 3. Why should they change their minds now? Their whole lives have been oriented around Unity. It's the only existence they know." The really striking part, he thought, is that so many people have flocked away from Unity, to this girl's father.

"But he *kills* people," Marion Fields said. "You said so; you said he has those hammer things he sends out."

"The Healers kill people too," Barris said.

"That's different." Her young, smooth face had on it an

absolute certitude. "It's because they have to. He wants to. Don't you see the difference?"

Barris thought, I was wrong. There is one thing, one institution, that she accepts without question. Her father. She had been doing for years what great numbers of people are now learning to do: follow Father Fields blindly, wherever he leads them.

"Where is your father?" he asked the girl. "I talked to him once; I'd like to talk to him again. You're in touch with him, aren't you?"

"No," she said.

"But you know where he could be found. You could get to him, if you wanted. For instance, if I let you go, you'd find your way to him. Isn't that so?" He could see by her evasive restlessness that he was right. He was making her very uncomfortable.

"What do you want to see him for?" Marion said.

"I have a proposal to make to him."

Her eyes widened, and then shone with slyness. "You're going to join the Movement, is that it? And you want him to promise that you'll be somebody important in it. Like he did—" She clapped her hand over her mouth and stared at him stricken. "Like he did," she finished, "with that other Director."

"Taubmann," Barris said. He lit a cigarette and sat smoking, facing the girl. It was peaceful down here beneath the ground, away from the frenzy and destruction going on above. And yet, he thought, I have to go back to it, as soon as possible. I'm here so I can do that. A sort of paradox. In this peaceful child's room I expect to find the solution to the most arduous task of all.

"You'll let me go if I take you to him?" Marion asked. "I can go free? I won't even have to go back to that school?"

"Of course. There's no reason to keep you."

"Mr. Dill kept me here."

Barris said, "Mr. Dill is dead."

"Oh," she said. She nodded slowly, somberly. "I see. That's too bad."

"I had the same feeling about him," Barris said. "At first I had no trust in what he said. He seemed to be making up a story to fool everyone. But oddly—" He broke off. Oddly, the man's story had not been spurious. Truthfulness did not seem to go naturally with a man like Jason Dill; he seemed to be created to tell—as Marion said—long public lies, while smiling constantly. Involved dogmatic accounts for the purpose of concealing the actual situation. And yet, when everything was out in the open, Jason Dill did not look so bad; he had not been so dishonest an official. Certainly, he had been trying to do his job. He had been loyal to the theoretical ideals of Unity . . . perhaps more so than anyone else.

Marion Fields said, "Those awful metal birds he's been making—those things he sends out that he kills people with. Can he make a lot of them?" She eyed him uneasily.

"Evidently there's no particular limit to what Vulcan 3 can produce. There's no restriction on raw materials available to him." *Him.* He, too, was saying that now. "And he has the technical know-how. He has more information available to him than any purely human agency in the world. And he's not limited by any ethical considerations."

In fact, he realized, Vulcan 3 is in an ideal position; his goal is dictated by logic, by relentless correct reasoning. It is no emotional bias or projection that motivates him to act as he does. So he will never suffer a change of heart, a conversion; he will never turn from a conqueror into a benevolent ruler.

"The techniques that Vulcan 3 will employ," Barris said to

the child gazing up at him, "will be brought into play according to the need. They'll vary in direct proportion to the problem facing him; if he has ten people opposed to him, he will probably employ some minor weapon, such as the original hammers equipped with heat beams. We've seen him use hammers of greater magnitude, equipped with chemical bombs; that's because the magnitude of his opposition has turned out to be that much greater. He meets whatever challenge exists."

Marion said, "So the stronger the Movement gets, the larger he'll grow. The stronger he'll become."

"Yes," Barris said. "And there's no point at which he'll have to stop; there's no known limit to his theoretical power and size."

"If the whole world was against him—"

"Then he'd have to grow and produce and organize to combat the whole world."

"Why?" she demanded.

"Because that's his job."

"He wants to?"

"No," Barris said. "He has to."

All at once, without any warning, the girl said, "I'll take you to him, Mr. Barris. My father, I mean."

Silently, Barris breathed a prayer of relief.

"But you have to come alone," she added instantly. "No guards or anybody with guns." Studying him she said, "You promise? On your word of honor?"

"I promise," Barris said.

Uncertainly, she said, "How'll we get there? He's in North America."

"By police cruiser. We have three of them up on the roof of the building. They used to belong to Jason Dill. When there's a lull in the attack, we'll take off."

"Can we get by the hammer birds?" she said, with a mixture of doubt and excitement.

"I hope so," Barris said.

As the Unity police cruiser passed low over New York City, Barris had an opportunity to see first-hand the damage which the Healers had done.

Much of the outlying business ring was in ruins. His own building was gone; only a heap of smoking rubble remained. Fires still burned out of control in the vast, sprawling rabbit warren that was—or had been—the residential section. Most of the streets were hopelessly blocked. Stores, he observed, had been broken into and looted.

But the fighting was over. The city was quiet. People roamed vaguely through the debris, picking about for valuables. Here and there brown-clad Healers organized repair and reclamation. At the sound of the jets of his police cruiser, the people below scattered for shelter. On the roof of an undestroyed factory building a blaster boomed at them inexpertly.

"Which way?" Barris said to the solemn child beside him.

"Keep going straight. We can land soon. They'll take us to him on foot." Frowning with worry, she murmured, "I hope they haven't changed it too much. I was at that school so long, and he was in that awful place, that Atlanta . . ."

Barris flew on. The open countryside did not show the same extensive injury that the big cities did; below him, the farms and even the small rural towns seemed about as they always had. In fact, there was more order in the hinterlands now than there had been before; the collapse of the rural Unity offices had brought about stability, rather than chaos. Local people, already committed to support of the Movement, had eagerly assumed the tasks of leadership.

"That big river," Marion said, straining to see. "There's a bridge. I see it." She shivered triumphantly. "Go by the bridge, and you'll see a road. When there's a junction with another road, put your ship down there." She gave him a radiant smile.

Several minutes later he was landing the police cruiser in an open field at the edge of a small Pennsylvania town. Before the jets were off, a truck had come rattling across the dirt and weeds, directly toward them.

This is it, Barris said to himself. It's too late to back out now.

The truck halted. Four men in overalls jumped down and came cautiously up to the cruiser. One of them waved a pellet-rifle. "Who are you?"

"Let me get out," Marion said to Barris. "Let me talk to them."

He touched the stud on the instrument panel which released the port; it slid open, and Marion at once scrambled out and hopped down to the dusty ground.

Barris, still in the ship, waited tensely while she conferred with the four men. Far up in the sky, to the north, a flock of hammers rushed inland, intent on business of their own. A few moments later bright fission flashes lit up the horizon. Vulcan 3 had apparently begun equipping his extensions with atomic tactical bombs.

One of the four men came up to the cruiser and cupped his hands to his mouth. "I'm Joe Potter. You're Barris?"

"That's right." Sitting in the ship, Barris kept his hand on his pencil beam. But, he realized, it was nothing more than a ritualistic gesture now; it had no practical importance.

"Say," Joe Potter said. "I'll take you to Father. If that's what you want, and she says it is. Come alone."

With the four men, Barris and Marion climbed aboard the ancient, dented truck. At once it started up; he was pitched from side to side as it swung around and started back the way it had come.

"By God," one of the men said, scrutinizing him. "You used to be North American Director. Didn't you?"

"Yes," Barris said.

The men mumbled among one another, and at last one of them slid over to Barris and said, "Listen, Mr. Barris." He shoved an envelope and a pencil at him. "Could I have your autograph?"

For an hour the truck headed along minor country roads, in the general direction of New York City. A few miles outside the demolished business ring, Potter halted the truck at a gasoline station. To the right of the station was a roadside café, a decrepit, weatherbeaten place. A few cars were pulled up in front of it. Some children were playing in the dirt by the steps, and a dog was tied up in the yard in the rear.

"Get out," Potter said. All four men seemed somewhat cross and taciturn from the long drive.

Barris got out slowly. "Where—"

"Inside." Potter started up the truck again. Marion hopped out to join Barris. The truck pulled away, made a turn, and disappeared back down the road in the direction from which they had just come.

Her eyes shining, Marion called, "Come on!" She scampered up on the porch of the café and tugged the door open. Barris followed after her, with caution.

In the dingy café, at a table littered with maps and papers, sat a man wearing a blue denim shirt and grease-stained work pants. An ancient audio-telephone was propped up beside him, next to a plate on which were the remains of a hamburger and fried potatoes. The man glanced up irritably, and Barris saw heavy ridged eyebrows, the irregular teeth, the penetrating glance that had so chilled him before, and which chilled him again now.

"I'll be darned," Father Fields said, pushing away his papers. "Look who's here."

"Daddy!" Marion cried; she leaped forward and threw her arms around him. "I'm so glad to see you—" Her words were cut off, smothered by the man's shirt as she pressed her face into it. Fields patted her on the back, oblivious to Barris.

Walking over to the counter, Barris seated himself alone. He remained there, meditating, until all at once he realized that Father Fields was addressing him. Glancing up, he saw the man's hand held out. Grinning, Fields shook hands with him.

"I thought you were in Geneva," Fields said. "It's nice seeing you again." His eyes traveled up and down Barris. "The one decent Director out of eleven. And we don't get you; we get practically the worst—barring Reynolds. We get that opportunist Taubmann." He shook his head ironically.

Barris said, "Revolutionary movements always draw opportunists."

"That's very charitable of you," Fields said. Reaching back, he drew up a chair and seated himself, tipping the chair until he was comfortable.

"Mr. Barris is fighting Vulcan 3," Marion declared, holding on tightly to her father's arm. "He's on our side."

"Oh, is that right?" Fields said, patting her. "Are you sure about that?"

She colored and stammered, "Well, anyhow, he's against Vulcan 3."

"Congratulations," Fields said to Barris. "You've made a wise choice. Assuming it's so."

Settling back against the counter, propping himself up on one elbow so that he, too, was comfortable, Barris said, "I came here to talk business with you."

In a leisurely, drawling voice, Fields said, "As you can see, I'm a pretty busy man. Maybe I don't have time to talk business."

"Find time," Barris said.

Fields said, "I'm not much interested in business. I'm more interested in work. You could have joined us back when it mattered, but you turned tail and walked out. Now—" He shrugged. "What the heck does it matter? Having you with us doesn't make any particular difference one way or another. We've pretty well won, now. I imagine that's why you've finally made up your mind which way you want to jump. Now you can see who's the winning side." He grinned once more, this time with a knowing, insinuating twinkle. "Isn't that so? You'd like to be on the winning side." He waggled his finger slyly at Barris.

"If I did," Barris said, "I wouldn't be here."

For a moment, Fields did not appear to understand. Then, by degrees, his face lost all humor; the bantering familiarity vanished. He became hard-eyed. "The hell you say," he said slowly. "Unity is gone, man. In a couple of days we swept the old monster system aside. What's there left? Those tricky businesses flapping around up there." He jerked his thumb, pointing upward. "Like the one I got, that day in the hotel, the one that came in the window looking for me. Did you ever get that? I patched it up pretty good and sent it on to you and your girl, for a—" He laughed. "A wedding present."

Barris said, "You've got nothing. You've destroyed nothing."

"Everything," Fields said in a grating whisper. "We've got everything there is, mister."

"You don't have Vulcan 3," Barris said. "You've got a lot of land; you blew up a lot of office buildings and recruited a lot of clerks and stenographers—that's all."

"We'll get him," Fields said, evenly.

"Not without your founder," Barris said. "Not now that he's dead."

Staring at Barris, Fields said, "My—" He shook his head slowly; his poise was obviously completely shattered. "What do you mean? I founded the Movement. I've headed it from the start."

Barris said, "I know that's a lie."

For a time there was silence.

"What does he mean?" Marion demanded, plucking anxiously at her father's arm.

"He's out of his mind," Fields said, still staring at Barris. The color had not returned to his face.

"You're an expert electrician," Barris said. "That was your trade. I saw your work on that hammer, your reconstruction. You're very good; in fact there probably isn't an electrician in the world today superior to you. You kept Vulcan 2 going all this time, didn't you?"

Fields' mouth opened and then shut. He said nothing.

"Vulcan 2 founded the Healers' Movement," Barris said.

"No," Fields said.

"You were only the fake leader. A puppet. Vulcan 2 created the Movement as an instrument to destroy Vulcan 3. That's why he gave Jason Dill instructions not to reveal the existence of the Movement to Vulcan 3; he wanted to give it time to grow."

# CHAPTER THIRTEEN

After a long time, Father Fields said, "Vulcan 2 was only a computing mechanism. It had no motives, no drives. Why would it act to impair Vulcan 3?"

"Because Vulcan 3 menaced it," Barris said. "Vulcan 2 was as much alive as Vulcan 3—no more and no less. It was created originally to do a certain job, and Vulcan 3 interfered with its doing that job, just as the withholding of data by Jason Dill interfered with Vulcan 3's doing its job."

"How did Vulcan 3 interfere with Vulcan 2's doing its job?" Father Fields said.

"By supplanting it," Barris said.

Fields said, "But I am the head of the Movement now. Vulcan 2 no longer exists." Rubbing his chin, he said, "There isn't a wire or a tube or a relay of Vulcan 2 intact."

"You did a thorough, professional job," Barris said.

The man's head jerked.

"You destroyed Vulcan 2," Barris said, "to keep Jason Dill from knowing. Isn't that so?"

"No," Fields said finally. "It isn't so. This is all a wild series of guesses on your part. You have no evidence; this is the typical insane slander generated by Unity. These mad charges, dreamed up and bolstered and embroidered—"

Once again, Barris noticed, the man had lost his regional accent. And his vocabulary, his use of words, had in this period of stress, greatly improved.

Marion Fields piped, "It's not true! My father founded the

Movement." Her eyes blazed with helpless, baffled fury at Barris. "I wish I hadn't brought you here."

"What evidence do you have?" Fields said.

"I saw the skill with which you rebuilt that ruined hammer," Barris said. "It amounted to mechanical genius on your part. With ability like that you could name your own job with Unity; there're no repairmen on my staff in New York capable of work like that. The normal use Unity would put you to with such ability would be servicing the Vulcan series. Obviously you know nothing about Vulcan 3—*and Vulcan 3 is self-servicing*. What does that leave but the older computers? And Vulcan 1 hasn't functioned in decades. And your age is such that, like Jason Dill, you would naturally have been a contemporary of Vulcan 2 rather—"

"Conjecture," Fields said.

"Yes," Barris admitted.

"Logic. Deduction. Based on the spurious premise that I had anything to do with any of the Vulcan series. Did it ever occur to you that there might have been alternate computers, designed by someone other than Nat Greenstreet, that competent crews might have been put to work at—"

From behind Barris a voice, a woman's voice, said sharply, "Tell him the truth, Father. Don't lie, for once."

Rachel Pitt came around to stand by Barris. Astonished to see her, Barris started to his feet.

"My two daughters," Fields said. He put his hand on Marion Fields' shoulder, and then, after a pause, he put his other hand on the shoulder of Rachel Pitt. "Marion and Rachel," he said to Barris. "The younger stayed with me, was loyal to me; the older had ambitions to marry a Unity man and live a well-to-do life with all the things that money can buy. She started to come back to me a couple of times. But did you really come back?" He gazed meditatively at Rachel Pitt. "I wonder. It doesn't sound like it."

Rachel said, "I'm loyal to you, Father. I just can't stand any more lies."

"I am telling the truth," Father Fields said in a harsh, bitter voice. "Barris accuses me of destroying Vulcan 2 to keep Jason Dill from knowing about the relationship between the old computer and the Movement. Do you think I care about Jason Dill? Did it ever matter what he knew? I destroyed Vulcan 2 because it wasn't running the Movement effectively; it was holding the Movement back, keeping it weak. It wanted the Movement to be nothing but an extension of itself, like those hammers of Vulcan 3. An instrument without life of its own."

His voice had gained power; his jaw jutted out and he confronted Barris and Rachel defiantly. The two of them moved involuntarily away from him, and closer to each other. Only Marion Fields remained with him.

"I freed the Movement," Fields said. "I freed humanity and made the Movement an instrument of human needs, human aspirations. Is that wicked?" He pointed his finger at Barris and shouted, "And before I'm finished I'm going to destroy Vulcan 3 as well, and free mankind from it, too. From both of them, first the older one and next the big one, the new one. Is that wrong? Are you opposed to that? If you are, then god damn it, go join them at the fortress; go join Reynolds."

Barris said, "It's a noble ideal, what you're saying. But you can't do it. It's impossible. Unless I help you."

Hunched forward in his chair, Father Fields said, "All right, Barris. You came here to do business. What's your deal?" Raising his head he said hoarsely, "What do you have to offer me?"

Barris said, "I know where the fortress is. I've been to it. Dill took me there. I can find it again. Without me, you'll never find it. At least, not in time; not before Vulcan 3 has developed such far-reaching offensive weapons that nothing will remain of life above ground."

"You don't think we'll find it?" Fields said.

"In fifteen months," Barris said, "you've failed to. Do you think you will in the next two weeks?"

Presently Father Fields said, "More like two years. We started looking from the very start." He shrugged. "Well, Director. What do you want in exchange?"

"Plenty," Barris said grimly. "I'll try to outline it as briefly as I can."

After Barris had finished, Father Fields was silent. "You want a lot," he said finally.

"That's right."

"It's incredible, you dictating terms to me. How many in your group?"

"Five or six."

Fields shook his head. "And there are millions of us, all over the world." From his pocket he produced a much-folded map; spreading it out on the counter he said, "We've taken over in America, in Eastern Europe, in all of Asia and Africa. It seemed only a question of time before we had the rest. We've been winning so steadily." He clenched his fist around a coffee mug on the counter and then suddenly grabbed it up and hurled it to the floor. The brown coffee oozed thickly out.

"Even if you did have sufficient time on your side," Barris said, "I doubt if you could ultimately have defeated Unity. It's hopeless to imagine that a grass-roots revolutionary movement can overthrow a modern bureaucratic system that's backed up with modern technology and elaborate industrial organization. A hundred years ago, your Movement might have worked. But times have changed. Government is a science conducted by trained experts."

Studying him with animosity, Fields said, "To win, you have to be on the inside."

"You have to know someone on the inside," Barris said. "And you do; you know me. I can get you in, where you will be able to attack the main trunk, not merely the branches."

"And the trunk," Fields said, "is Vulcan 3. Give us credit for knowing that, at least. That thing has always been our target." He let out his breath raggedly. "All right, Barris; I agree to your terms."

Barris felt himself relax. But he kept his expression under control. "Fine," he said.

"You're surprised, aren't you?" Fields said.

"No," he said. "Relieved. I thought possibly you might fail to see how precarious your position is."

Bringing forth a pocket watch, Fields examined it. "What do you want for the attack on the fortress? Weapons are still in short supply with us. We're mainly oriented around man power."

"There are weapons back at Geneva."

"How about transportation?"

"We have three high-speed military cruisers; they'll do." Barris wrote rapidly on a piece of paper. "A small concentrated attack by skillful men—experts hitting at the vital center. A hundred well-chosen men will do. Everything depends on the first ten minutes in the fortress; if we succeed, it'll be right away. There will be no second chance."

Fields gazed at him intently. "Barris, do you really think we have a chance? Can we really get to Vulcan 3?" His grease-stained hands twisted. "For years I've thought of nothing else. Smashing that satanic mass of parts and tubes—"

"We'll get to him," Barris said.

Fields collected the men that Barris needed. They were loaded into the cruiser, and Barris at once headed back toward Geneva, Fields accompanying him.

Halfway across the Atlantic they passed an immense swarm of hammers streaking toward helpless, undefended North America. These were quite large, almost as large as the cruiser. They moved with incredible speed, disappearing almost at once. A few minutes later a new horde appeared, these like slender needles. They ignored the ship and followed the first group over the horizon.

"New types," Barris said. "He's wasting no time."

The Unity Control Building was still in friendly hands. They landed on the roof and hurried down the ramps into the building. On orders from Fields, the Healers had ceased attacking. But now hammers swarmed constantly overhead, diving down and twisting agilely to avoid the roof guns. Half of the main structure was in ruins, but the guns fired on, bringing down the hammers when they came too close.

"It's a losing battle," Daily muttered. "We're short on ammunition. There seem to be an endless number of the damn things."

Barris worked rapidly. He supplied his attack force with the best weapons available, supplies stored in the vaults below the Control Building. From the five Directors he selected Pegler and Chai, and a hundred of the best-trained troops.

"I'm going along," Fields said. "If the attack fails I don't want to stay alive. If it succeeds I want to be part of it."

Barris carefully uncrated a manually operated fission bomb. "This is for him." He weighed the bomb in the palm of his hand; it was no larger than an onion. "My assumption is that they'll admit me and possibly Chai and Pegler. We can probably persuade them that we're coming over to rejoin Unity. At least we'll be able to get part of the distance in."

"Anyhow you hope so," Fields said curtly.

At sunset, Barris loaded the three cruisers with the men and equipment. The roof guns sent up a heavy barrage to cover their take-off. Hammers in action nearby at once began following the ships as they rose into the sky.

"We'll have to shake them," Barris said. He gave quick orders. The three cruisers shot off in different directions, dividing up rapidly. A few hammers tagged them awhile and then gave up.

"I'm clear," Chai in the second cruiser reported.

"Clear," Pegler in the third said.

Barris glanced at the older man beside him. Behind them the ship was crowded with tense, silent soldiers, loaded down with weapons, squatting nervously in a mass as the ship raced through the darkness. "Here we go," Barris said. He swung the ship in a wide arc. Into the communications speaker he ordered, "We'll re-form for the attack. I'll lead. You two come behind."

"Are we close?" Fields asked, a queer expression on his face.

"Very." Barris studied the ship's controls. "We should be over it in a moment. Get set."

Barris dived. Pegler's ship whipped through the darkness behind him, lashing toward the ground below; Chai's ship shot off to the right and headed directly over the fortress.

Hammers rose in vast swarms and moved toward Chai's ship, separating and engulfing it.

"Hang on," Barris gasped.

The ground rose; landing brakes screamed. The ship hit, spinning and crashing among the trees and boulders.

"Out!" Barris ordered, pulling himself to his feet and throwing the hatch release. The hatches slid back and the men poured out, dragging their equipment into the cold night darkness.

Above them in the sky, Chai's ship fought with the hammers; it twisted and rolled, firing rapidly. More hammers rose from the fortress, great black clouds that swiftly gained altitude. Pegler's ship was landing. It roared over them and crashed against the side of a hill a few hundred yards from the other defense wall of the fortress.

The heavy guns of the fortress were beginning to open up. A vast fountain of white burst loose, showering rocks and debris on Barris and Fields as they climbed out of their ship.

"Hurry," Barris said. "Get the bores going."

The men were assembling two gopher bores. The first had already whined into action. More tactical atomic shells from the fortress struck near them; the night was lit up with explosions.

Barris crouched down. "How are you making out?" he shouted above the racket, his lips close to his helmet speaker.

"All right," Pegler's voice said weakly in his earphones. "We're down and getting out the big stuff."

"That'll hold off the hammers," Barris said to Fields. He peered up at the sky. "I hope Chai—"

Chai's ship rolled and spun, trying to evade the ring of hammers closing around it. Its jets smoked briefly. A direct hit. The ship wobbled and hesitated.

"Drop your men," Barris ordered into his phones. "You're right over the fortress."

From Chai's ship showered a cloud of white dots. Men in

jump suits, drifting slowly toward the ground below. Hammers screeched around them; the men fired back with pencil beams. The hammers retreated warily.

"Chai's men will take care of the direct attack," Barris explained. "Meanwhile, the bores are moving."

"Umbrella almost ready," a technician reported.

"Good. They're beginning to dive on us; their screenprobes must have spotted us."

The fleets of screaming hammers were descending, hurtling toward the ground. Their beams stabbed into the trees and ignited columns of flaming wood and branches. One of Pegler's cannons boomed. A group of hammers disappeared, but more took their places. An endless torrent of hammers, rising up from the fortress like black bats.

The umbrella flickered purple. Reluctantly, it came on and settled in place. Vaguely, beyond it, Barris could make out the hammers circling in confusion. A group of them entered the umbrella and were silently puffed out.

Barris relaxed. "Good. Now we don't have to worry about them."

"Gophers are halfway along," the leader of the bore team reported.

Two immense holes yawned, echoing and vibrating as the gopher bores crept into the earth. Technicians disappeared after them. The first squad of armed troops followed them cautiously, swallowed up by the earth.

"We're on our way," Barris said to Fields.

Standing off by himself, Father Fields surveyed the trees, the line of hills in the distance. "No visible sign of the fortress," he murmured. "Nothing to give it away." He seemed deep in thought, as if barely aware of the battle in progress. "This forest . . . the perfect place. I would never have known." Turning, he walked toward Barris.

Seeing the look on the man's face, Barris felt deep uneasiness. "What is it?" he said.

Fields said, "I've been here before."

"Yes," Barris said.

"Thousands of times. I worked here most of my life." The man's face was stark. "This is where Vulcan 2 used to be." His hands jerked aimlessly. "This was where I came to destroy Vulcan 2." Nodding his head at a massive moss-covered boulder, he said, "I walked by that. To the service ramp. They didn't even know the ramp still existed; it was declared obsolete years ago. Abandoned and shut off. But I knew about it." His voice rose wildly. "I can come and go any time I want; I have constant access to that place. *I know a thousand ways to get down there.*"

Barris said, "But you didn't know that Vulcan 3 was down there, too. At the deepest level. They didn't acquaint your crew with—"

"I didn't know Jason Dill," Fields said. "I wasn't in a position to meet him as an equal. As you were."

"So now you know," Barris said.

"You gave me nothing," Fields said. "You had nothing to tell me that I didn't know already." Coming slowly toward Barris he said in a low voice, "I could have figured it out, in time. Once we had tried every other place—" In his hand a pencil beam appeared, gripped tightly.

Keeping himself calm, Barris said, "But you still won't get in, Father. They'll never let you in. They'll kill you long before you penetrate all the way to Vulcan 3. You'll have to depend on me." Pointing to his sleeve, he indicated his Director's stripe. "Once I get in there I can walk up and down those corridors; no one will stop me, because they're part of the same structure I'm part of. And I'm in a position of authority equal to any of them, Reynolds included."

Fields said, "Any of them—except for Vulcan 3."

Off to the right, Pegler's cannon thundered as the fleets of hammers turned their attention on them. The hammers dived and released bombs. An inferno of white pillars checkered across the countryside, moving toward Pegler's ship.

"Get your umbrella up!" Barris shouted into his helmet speaker.

Pegler's umbrella flickered. It hesitated—

A small atomic bomb cut across dead center. Pegler's ship vanished; clouds of particles burst into the air, metal and ash showering over the flaming ground. The heavy cannon ceased abruptly.

"It's up to us," Barris said.

Over the fortress the first of Chai's men had reached the ground. The defense guns spun around, leaving Barris' ship and focusing on the drifting dots.

"They don't have a chance," Fields muttered.

"No." Barris started toward the first of the two tunnels. "But we have." Ignoring the pencil beam in the older man's hand, he continued, his back to Fields.

Abruptly the fortress shuddered. A vast tongue of fire rolled across it. The surface fused in an instant; the wave of molten metal had sealed over the fortress.

"They cut themselves off," Barris said. "They've closed down." He shook himself into motion and entered the tunnel, squeezing past the power leads to the gopher.

An ugly cloud of black rolled up from the sea of glimmering slag that had been the surface of the fortress. The hammers fluttered above it uncertainly, cut off from the levels beneath.

Barris made his way along the tunnel, pushing past the technicians operating the gopher. The gopher rumbled and vibrated as it cut through the layers of clay and rock toward the fortress. The air was hot and moist. The men worked feverishly, directing the gopher deeper and deeper. Torrents of steaming water poured from the clay around them.

"We must be close," Fields' voice came to him, from behind.

"We should emerge near the deepest level," Barris said. He did not look to see if the pencil beam was still there; he kept on going.

The gopher shrieked. Its whirring noise tore into metal; the bore team urged it forward. The gopher slashed into a wall of steel and reinforced stressed plastic and then slowed to a stop.

"We're there," Barris said.

The gopher shuddered. Gradually it inched forward. The leader of the team leaned close to Barris. "The other gopher's through, into the fortress. But they don't know exactly where."

All at once the wall collapsed inward. Liquid steel pelted them, sizzling. The soldiers moved ahead, pushing through the gap. Barris and Fields hurried with them. The jagged metal seared them as they squeezed through. Barris stumbled and fell, rolling in the boiling water and debris.

Putting his pencil beam away, Fields pulled him to his feet. They glanced at each other, neither of them speaking. And then they looked about them, at the great corridor that stretched out, lit by the recessed lighting familiar to both of them.

The lowest level of the fortress!

# CHAPTER FOURTEEN

A few astonished Unity guards scampered toward them, tugging a blast cannon inexpertly into position.

Barris fired. From behind him, pencil beams cut past him toward the cannon. The cannon fired once, crazily. The roof of the corridor dissolved; clouds of ash rolled around them. Barris moved forward. Now the blast cannon was in ruins. The Unity guards were pulling back, firing as they retreated.

"Mine crew," Barris snapped.

The mine crew advanced and released their sucker mines. The mines leaped down the corridor toward the retreating Unity guards. At the sight the guards broke and fled; the mines exploded, hurling streamers of flame against the walls.

"Here we go," Barris said. Crouching, he hurried along the corridor, clutching the fission bomb tight. Beyond a turn the Unity guards were shutting an emergency lock.

"Get them!" Barris shouted.

Fields ran past him, galloping in long-legged strides, his arms windmilling. His pencil beam traced a ribbon of ash across the surface of the lock; intricate bits of mechanism flew into the air. Behind the lock Unity teams were bringing up more mobile cannons. A few hammers fluttered around their heads, screaming instructions.

Following Fields, Barris reached the lock. Their men swarmed past them, firing into the narrow breach. A hammer sailed out, straight at Barris; he caught a vision of glittering metal eyes, clutching claws—and then the hammer winked out, caught by a pencil beam.

Fields seated himself on the floor by the hinge-rim of the lock. His expert fingers traced across the impulse leads. A sudden flash. The lock trembled and sagged. Barris threw his weight against it. The lock gave. Gradually it slid back, leaving a widened gap.

"Get in," Barris ordered.

His men poured through, crashing against the barricade hastily erected by the Unity guards. Hammers dived on them frantically, smashing at their heads.

Pushing past, Barris glanced around. A series of corridors twisted off in different directions. He hesitated.

*Can I do it?* he asked himself.

Taking a deep, unsteady breath, he sprinted away from Fields and the soldiers, along a side corridor. The sound of fighting died as he raced up a ramp. A door slid open automatically for him; as it shut behind him he slowed, panting.

A moment later he was walking briskly along a passage, in the silence far away from the hectic activity. He came to an elevator, halted, and touched a stud. The elevator at once made itself available to him. Entering, he permitted it to carry him upward.

This is the only way, he told himself. He forced himself to remain calm as the elevator carried him farther and farther away from Vulcan 3 and the scene of the activity. *No direct assault will work.*

At an upper level he stopped the elevator and stepped out.

A group of Unity officials stood about, conferring. Clerks and executives. Gray-clad men and women who glanced at him briefly or not at all. He caught a glimpse of office doors . . . without pausing, he began to walk.

He came presently onto a foyer, from which branched several corridors. Behind a turnstile sat a robot checker, inactive; no one was using its facilities. At the presence of Barris it lit up.

"Credentials, sir," it said.

"Director," he said, displaying his stripe.

Ahead of him the turnstile remained fixed. "This portion of the area is classified," the robot said. "What is your business and by whose authority are you attempting to enter?"

Barris said sharply, "My own authority. Open up; this is urgent."

It was his tone that the robot caught, rather than the words. The turnstile rattled aside; the habitual pattern of the assembly, its robot controller included, had been activated as it had been many times in the past. "Pardon intrusion into urgent business, Director," the robot said, and at once shut off; its light died.

Back to sleep, Barris thought grimly.

He continued on until he came to an express descent ramp. At once he stepped onto it; the ramp plunged, and he was on his way back down again. To the bottom level—and Vulcan 3.

Several guards stood about in the corridor as Barris stepped from the ramp. They glanced at him and started to come to attention. Then one of them gave a convulsive grimace; his hand fumbled stupidly at his belt.

Bringing out his pencil beam, Barris fired. The guard, headless, sank to one side and then collapsed; the other guards stared in disbelief, paralyzed.

"Traitor," Barris said. "Right here, in our midst."

The guards gaped at him.

"Where's Director Reynolds?" Barris said.

Gulping, one of the guards said, "In office six, sir. Down that way." Half pointing, he bent over the remains of his companion; the others gathered around.

"Can you get him out here for me?" Barris demanded. "Or am I supposed to go search him up?"

One of the guards murmured, "If you want to wait here, sir . . ."

"Wait here, hell," Barris said. "Are we all supposed to stand around while they break in and slaughter us? You know they're through in two places—they have those gopher bores going."

While the guards stammered out some sort of answer, he turned and strode off in the direction that the guard had indicated.

No Unity minion, he said to himself, will ever argue with a Director; it might cost him his job.

Or, in this case, his life.

As soon as the guards were out of sight behind him he turned off the corridor. A moment later he came out into a well-lighted major artery. The floor beneath his feet hummed and vibrated, and as he walked along he felt the intensity of action increase.

He was getting close, now. The center of Vulcan 3 was not far off.

The passage made an abrupt turn to the right. He followed, and found himself facing a young T-class official and two guards. All three men were armed. They seemed to be in the process of pushing a metal cart loaded with punchcards; he identified the cards as a medium by which data were presented, under certain circumstances, to the Vulcan computers. This official, then, was part of the feed-teams.

"Who are you?" Barris said, before the young official could speak. "What's your authority for being in this area? Let's see written permission."

The young official said, "My name is Larson, Director. I was directly responsible to Jason Dill before his death." Eyeing Barris, he smiled respectfully and said, "I saw you several times with Mr. Dill, sir. When you were here involving the reconstruction of Vulcan 2."

"I believe I noticed you," Barris said.

Pushing his cart along, Larson said, "I have to feed these at once to Vulcan 3; with your permission I'll go along. How's the fighting going on above? Someone says they've broken in somewhere. I heard a lot of noise." Clearly agitated, but concerned only with his clearly laid-out task, Larson continued, "Amazing how active Vulcan 3 is, after being inactive for so many months. He's come up with quite a number of effective weapons to deal with the situation."

Glancing at Barris shrewdly, he said, "Isn't it probable that Reynolds will be the new Managing Director? His able prosecution of Dill, the way he exposed the various—" He broke off in order to manipulate the combination of a huge set of barrier-doors. The doors swung open—

And there, ahead of Barris, was a vast chamber. At the far end he saw a wall of metal, perfectly blank. The side of a cube, one part of something that receded into the structure of the building; he caught only a glimpse of it, an impression.

"There it is," Larson said to him. "Peaceful here, in comparison to what's going on above ground. You wouldn't think he— I mean, it—had anything to do with the action against the Healers. And yet it's all being directed from here." He and his two guards pushed the cart of data-cards forward. "Care to come closer?" Larson asked Barris; showing him that he knew everything of importance. "You can watch the way the data are fed. It's quite interesting."

Passing by Barris, Larson began directing the removal of the cards; he had the guards load up with them. Standing behind the three men, Barris reached into his coat. His fingers closed over the onion-shaped object.

As he drew the fission bomb out, he saw, on Larson's sleeve, a shiny metal bug; it clung there, riding along, its antennae quivering. For a moment Barris thought, It's an insect. Some natural life form that brushed against him when he was above ground, in the forest.

The shiny metal bug flew up into the air. He heard the high-frequency whine as it passed him, and knew it then. A tiny hammer, a version of the basic type. For observation. It had been aware of him from the moment Larson encountered him.

Seeing him staring at the bug as it zipped away from them, Larson said, "Another one. There's been one hanging around me all day. It was clinging to my work smock for a while." He added, "Vulcan 3 uses them for relaying messages. I've seen a number of them around."

From the tiny hammer an ear-splitting squeal dinned out at the two men. *"Stop him! Stop him at once!"*

Larson blinked in bewilderment.

Holding onto the bomb, Barris strode toward the face of Vulcan 3. He did not run; he walked swiftly and silently.

*"Stop him, Larson!"* the hammer shrilled. *"He's here to destroy me! Make him get away from me!"*

Gripping the bomb tightly, Barris began to run.

A pencil beam fired past him; he crouched and ran on, zigzagging back and forth.

*"If you let him destroy me you'll destroy the world!"* A second tiny hammer appeared, dancing in the air before Barris. *"Madman!"*

He heard, from other parts of the chamber, the abuse piping at him from other mobile extensions. *"Monster!"*

Again a heat beam slashed past him; he half-fell, and, drawing out his own pencil, turned and fired directly back. He saw a brief scene: Larson with the two guards, firing at him in confusion, trying not to hit the wall of Vulcan 3. His own beam touched one of the guards; he ceased firing at once and fell writhing.

*"Listen to me!"* a full-sized hammer blared, skipping into the chamber and directly at Barris. In desperate fury the hammer crashed at him, missing him and bursting apart against the concrete floor, its pieces spewing over him.

*"While there's still time!"* another took up. *"Get him away, feed-team leader! He's killing me!"*

With his pencil beam, Barris shot down a hammer as it emerged above him; he had not seen it come into the chamber. The hammer, only damaged, fluttered down. Struggling toward him, across the floor, it screeched, *"We can agree! We can come to an arrangement!"*

On and on he ran.

*"This can be negotiated! There is no basic disagreement!"*

Raising his arm, he hurled the bomb.

*"Barris! Barris! Please do not—"*

From the intricate power supply of the bomb came a faint *pop*. Barris threw himself down, his arms over his face. An ocean of white light lapped up at him, picking him up and sweeping him away.

I got it, he thought. I was successful.

A monstrous hot wind licked at him as he drifted; he skidded on, along with the wind. Debris and flaming rubbish burst over and around him. A surface far away hurtled at him. He doubled up, his head averted, and then he flew through the surface; it split and gave way, and he went on, tumbling into darkness, swept on by the tides of wind and heat.

His last thought was, *It was worth it. Vulcan 3 is dead!*

———

Father Fields sat watching a hammer. The hammer wobbled. It hesitated in its frantic, aimless flight. And then it spiraled to the floor.

One by one, dropping silently, the hammers crashed down and lay still. Inert heaps of metal and plastic, nothing more. Without motion. Their screeching voices had ceased.

What a relief, he said to himself.

Getting to his feet he walked shakily over to the four medical corpsmen. "How is he?" he said.

Without looking up, the corpsman said, "We're making progress. His chest was extensively damaged. We've plugged in an exterior heart-lung system, and it's giving rapid assistance." The semiautomatic surgical tools crept across the body of William Barris, exploring, repairing. They seemed to have virtually finished with the chest; now they had turned their attention to his broken shoulder.

"We'll need boneforms," one of the corpsmen said. Glancing around he said, "We don't have any here with us. He'll have to be flown back to Geneva."

"Fine," Fields said. "Get him started."

The litter slid expertly under Barris and began lifting him.

"That traitor," a voice beside Fields said.

He turned his head and saw Director Reynolds standing there, gazing at Barris. The man's clothing was torn, and over his left eye was a deep gash. Fields said, "You're out of a job now."

With absolute bitterness, Reynolds said, "And so are you. What becomes of the great crusade, now that Vulcan 3 is gone? Do you have any other constructive programs to offer?"

"Time will tell," Fields said. He walked along beside the litter as it carried Barris up the ramp to the waiting ship.

"You did very well," Fields said. He lit a cigarette and placed it between Barris' parted lips. "Better not start talking. Those surgical robots are still fussing over you." He indicated the several units at work on the man's ruined shoulder.

"Do any of the computing components of Vulcan 3 . . ." Barris murmured weakly.

"Some survived," Fields said. "Enough for your purposes. You can add and subtract, anyhow, using what's left." Seeing the worry on the injured man's face he said, "I'm joking. A great deal survived. Don't worry. They can patch up the parts you want. As a matter of fact, I can probably lend a hand. I still have some skill."

"The structure of Unity will be different," Barris said.

"Yes," Fields said.

"We'll broaden our base. We have to."

Fields gazed out of the ship's window, ignoring the injured man. At last Barris gave up trying to talk. His eyes shut; Fields took the cigarette as it rolled from the man's lips onto his shirt.

"We'll talk later," Fields said, finishing the cigarette himself.

The ship droned on, in the direction of Geneva.

Looking out at the empty sky, Fields thought, Nice not to see those things flying around. When one died they all died. Strange, to realize that we've seen our last one . . . the last hammer to go buzzing, screeching about, attacking and bombing, laying waste wherever it goes.

Kill the trunk, as Barris had said.

The man was right about a lot of things, Fields said to himself. He was the only one who could have gotten all the way in; they did manage to stop the rest of us. The attack bogged down, until those things stopped flying. And then it didn't matter.

I wonder if he's right about the rest?

———

In the hospital room at Geneva, Barris sat propped up in bed, facing Fields. "What information can you give me on the analysis of the remains?" he said. "I have a hazy memory of the trip here; you said that most of the memory elements survived."

"You're so anxious to rebuild it," Fields said.

"As an instrument," Barris said. "Not a master. That was the agreement between us. You have to permit a continuation of rational use of machines. None of this emotional 'scrap the machines' business. None of your Movement slogans."

Fields nodded. "If you really think you can keep control in the right hands. In our hands. I have nothing against machines as such; I was very fond of Vulcan 2. Up to a point."

"At that point," Barris said, "you demolished it."

The two men regarded each other.

"I'll keep hands off," Fields said. "It's a fair deal. You delivered; you got in there and blew the thing up. I admit that."

Barris grunted, but said nothing.

"You'll put an end to the cult of the technocrat?" Fields said. "For experts only—run by and *for* those oriented around verbal knowledge; I'm so damn sick of that. Mind stuff—as if manual skills like bricklaying and pipe-fitting weren't worth talking about. As if all the people who work with their hands, the skill of their fingers—" He broke off. "I'm tired of having those people looked down on."

Barris said, "I don't blame you."

"We'll cooperate," Fields said. "With you priests in gray—as we've been calling you in our pamphlets. But take care. If the aristocracy of slide rules and pastel ties and polished black shoes starts to get out of hand again . . ." He pointed at the street far below the window. "You'll hear us out there again."

"Don't threaten me," Barris said quietly.

Fields flushed. "I'm not threatening you. I'm pointing out the facts to you. If we're excluded from the ruling elite, *why should we cooperate?*"

There was silence then.

"What do you want done about Atlanta?" Barris said finally.

"We can agree on that," Fields said. He flipped his cigarette away; bending, he retrieved it and crushed it out. "I want to see that place taken apart piece by piece. Until it's a place to keep cows. A pasture land. With plenty of trees."

"Good," Barris said.

"Can my daughter come in for a while?" Fields said. "Rachel. She'd like to talk to you."

"Maybe later," Barris said. "I still have a lot of things to work out in my mind."

"She wants you to start action going against Taubmann for that slanderous letter he wrote about you. The one she was blamed for." He hesitated. "Do you want my opinion?"

"Okay," Barris said.

Fields said, "I think there ought to be an amnesty. To end that stuff once and for all. Keep Taubmann on or retire him from the system. But let's have an end of accusations. Even true ones."

"Even a correct suspicion," Barris said, "is still a suspicion."

Showing his relief, Fields said, "We all have plenty to do. Plenty of rebuilding. We'll have enough on our hands."

"Too bad Jason Dill isn't here to admonish us," Barris said. "He'd enjoy writing out the directives and public presentations of the reconstruction work." Suddenly he said, "You were working for Vulcan 2 and Dill was working for Vulcan 2. You were both carrying out its policies toward Vulcan 3. Do you think Vulcan 2 was jealous of Vulcan 3? They may have been mechanical constructs, but as far as we were concerned they had all the tendencies of two contending entities—each out to get the other."

Fields murmured, "And each lining up supporters. Following your analysis . . ." He paused, his face dark with introspection.

"Vulcan 2 won," Barris said.

"Yes." Fields nodded. "He—or it—got virtually all of us lined up on one side, with Vulcan 3 on the other. We ganged up on Vulcan 3." He laughed sharply. "Vulcan 3's logic was absolutely right; there was a vast worldwide conspiracy directed against it, and to preserve itself it had to invent and develop and produce one weapon after another. And still it was destroyed. Its paranoid suspicions were founded in fact."

Like the rest of Unity, Barris thought. Vulcan 3, like Dill and myself, Rachel Pitt and Taubmann—all drawn into the mutual accusations and suspicions and near-pathological system-building.

"Pawns," Fields was saying. "We humans—god damn it, Barris; we were pawns of those two things. They played us off against one another, like inanimate pieces. The things became alive and the living organisms were reduced to things. Everything was turned inside out, like some terrible morbid view of reality."

Standing at the doorway of the hospital room, Rachel Pitt said in a low voice, "I hope we can get out from under that morbid view." Smiling timidly, she came toward Barris and her father. "I don't want to press any legal action against Taubmann; I've been thinking it over."

Either that, Barris thought, or making it a point to listen in on other people's conversations. But he said nothing aloud.

"How long do you think it will take?" Fields said, studying him acutely. "The *real* reconstruction—not the buildings and roads, but the minds. Distrust and mutual suspicion have been bred into us since childhood; the schools started it going on us—they forced out characters. We can't shake it overnight."

He's right, Barris thought. It's going to be hard. And it's going to take a long time. Possibly generations.

But at least the living elements, the human beings, had survived. And the mechanical ones had not. That was a good sign, a step in the right direction.

Across from him, Rachel Pitt was smiling less timidly, with more assurance now. Coming over to him, she bent down and touched him reassuringly on the plastic film that covered his shoulder. "I hope you'll be up and around soon," she said.

He considered that a good sign too.

### LIES, INC.

In this wry, paranoid vision of the future, overpopulation has turned cities into cramped industrial anthills. For those sick of this dystopian reality, one corporation, Trails of Hoffman, Inc., promises an alternative: Take a teleport to Whale's Mouth, a colonized planet billed as the supreme paradise. The only catch is that you can never come back. When a neurotic man named Rachmael ben Applebaum discovers that the promotional films of happy crowds cheering their newfound existence on Whale's Mouth were faked, he decides to pilot a spaceship on the eighteen-year journey there to see if anyone wants to return.

Fiction/Science Fiction/1-4000-3008-0

### FLOW MY TEARS, THE POLICEMAN SAID

Television star Jason Taverner is so famous that thirty million viewers eagerly watch his prime-time show until one day, all proof of his existence is erased. And in the claustrophobic betrayal state of *Flow My Tears, the Policeman Said*, loss of proof is synonymous with loss of life. As Taverner races to solve the riddle of his "disappearance" the author immerses us in a horribly plausible United States in which everyone informs on everyone else, a world in which even the omniscient police have something to hide. His bleakly beautiful novel bores into the deepest bedrock of the self and plants a stick of dynamite at its center.

Fiction/Science Fiction/0-679-74066-X

### EYE IN THE SKY

While sightseeing at the Belmont Bevatron, Jack Hamilton, along with seven others, is caught in a lab accident. When he regains consciousness, he finds himself in a fantasy world of Old Testament morality gone awry—a place of instant plagues, immediate damnations, and death to all perceived infidels. Hamilton figures out how he and his compatriots can escape this world and return to their own, but first they must pass through three other vividly fantastical worlds, each more perilous and hilarious than the one before.

Fiction/Science Fiction/1-4000-3010-2